Helen's Adventures

Helen's Adventures

A Kinky Companions Novella

Alex Markson

This paperback edition 2020

First published by Parignon Press 2020

Copyright © Alex Markson 2020

Alex Markson asserts the moral right to be identified as the author of this work in accordance with the Copyright, Designs and Patents Act 1988

ISBN: 979 8 58 050290 8

Chapter 1 - Beginnings

My name is Helen.

At least, that is how everyone knows me now. I was christened Annabelle Helena Charlotte Giselle. Something of a mouthful, and a waste of time really because almost from birth, everyone called me Bella.

My mother was a single parent and not a particularly good one. If that sounds harsh, I'll explain. We lived in a comfortable mews house in St John's Wood in London. It wasn't huge, but I came to realise as I grew up it was somewhere many people could only dream of. My earliest memories are of being in the house, feeling lonely.

When I started school at a local primary, I was overwhelmed by so many other children. I'd spent my early years alone with my mother, she didn't seem to have any friends. At the time, it seemed perfectly normal to me. The only other people in my life were an occasional babysitter, and a kindly uncle called Allan.

When I was invited to the homes of other children, my mother nearly always declined. None were ever invited to visit us. By the age of eight, I was beginning to see how different my life was to the other kids at school. But before I was able to rationalise any questions to ask my mother, my life changed dramatically.

I was sent off to boarding school. A small girl's school in Kent in an old manor house set in large, unkempt gardens. The sort of establishment found all over the country at the time, but which have fallen by the wayside in the intervening years.

There were less than a hundred girls between the ages of eight and eleven, and I hated it at first. Too much noise, too much activity. There was nowhere to hide, nowhere to be quiet. The dormitories were always a cacophony of screams, laughs, and giggles. To begin with, I cried myself to sleep every night, but I soon discovered I wasn't the only one. Slowly, I made friends. We supported each other, helped each other.

Once again, when we talked about our families, mine seemed different. There were other girls who lived with their mothers. I learned about divorce and step-parents, although our understanding of these things at the age of eight or nine wasn't wholly accurate. But I realised how isolated my mother and I were.

At the end of the first term, I asked my mother about my father. I'd asked before, but she'd been evasive. 'He's not around anymore,' or 'you don't want to know.' Never a complete answer, and so began a source of bitterness between us which grew and festered as I got older.

During the school holidays, Uncle Allan visited us regularly. He always made me laugh and one day I found out why. I saw him on television. It turned out Uncle Allan was a famous actor. Films, television, and the stage. A popular leading man, generally veering towards the light and comedic.

Occasionally, he would take my mother and me to a café or restaurant. He always introduced us to friends and fans, and I basked in the recognition he received.

Back at school, I had a small circle of friends now, but the weekends were difficult. Most of the girls came from wealthy families, and the school allowed us to invite friends home to stay two or three times a term. I was invited a few times, but my mother wouldn't return the favour, so I wasn't invited a second time.

Except by Caroline's mother. Caroline was my best friend; a slightly dramatic girl, who could talk her way out of any situation with the straightest of faces. I thought she was wonderful. When she first invited me to go home with her for the weekend, I was scared. I'd never stayed with a friend; I didn't know what was expected.

Her father was in the army, so I never met him, but her mother was a friendly woman and, I think, felt I was good for Caroline. Although I could never invite her to stay, I visited her home several times. It was her mother who persuaded me to accept a feature I'd always hated. My hair.

I had red hair. Not slightly ginger, or reddish. But RED. A colour which many people over the years have thought is artificial. It wasn't just the colour. It was also thick and wavy, impossible to do much with. In an era when hairstyles tended to be highly styled and sculpted, I felt deeply unfashionable.

I tended to tame it within an inch of its life and tie it up or band it, trying to hide it. It got me more than my fair share of nasty comments and finger-pointing.

One weekend, when I was staying with Caroline, her mother happened to mention my hair. But she was so positive about it, envious, even. I told her I hated it. She sat down with me and asked why. I tried to explain, but she undid all my bands and brushed it out. It was already long; my mother had forbidden me to have it cut short. When she finished, she made me look at it in the mirror. I was so self-conscious about it, I hardly ever did that.

She told me it was okay to be different, okay to stand out. You didn't have to fit in. It was something of an epiphany for me. I know it sounds ridiculous, but my attitude to my hair changed from that moment. I still wasn't totally happy with it, but I no longer tried to hide it.

It was all change again at eleven. I moved to another school; a proper, regimented private school for girls. I loved it. I enjoyed routine, rules, and timetables. A lot of the girls were there because their rich families were hoping a private education might knock some sense into their less than clever daughters. Some hope. I wasn't the brightest, but I was intelligent enough to keep ahead of the pack.

My relationship with my mother was distant now. We hardly communicated at all, perhaps two letters each over the course of a term. During the holidays, I went home, but she was often out, thinking me old enough now to be on my own. We tolerated one another. I began to realise she drank but didn't understand the reasons or consequences.

I was happier at school and did well. Ten O-levels followed, and I sat four A-levels, expecting good grades; university beckoned. Then fate intervened.

A few days after sitting my exams, a teacher came to find me and took me to the headmistress's office. There, I found my mother. She was in a daze.

"Uncle Allan's dead," she said. "I've come to take you home."

I was stunned. Now in a daze myself, I packed all my stuff and we drove back to London. Not a word was said during the whole two-hour journey.

At home, my mother started drinking. I didn't know what to do. I asked her what had happened, but all I got was her repeating Allan was dead. I couldn't get any details; couldn't understand why not. I'd not experienced grief but was upset my uncle had died. He'd been a part of my whole life, a regular visitor and kind man. I presumed it was worse for her, having lost a brother. But it all changed when she got really drunk.

I tried to comfort her, but she kept pushing me away. Her mood was almost angry, and I was confused.

"Mum, I'm sad too. I loved Uncle Allan."

She gave me a pitying look.

"You don't get it, do you?"

"Get what?"

"Uncle Allan," she said, sneering. "Uncle Allan ..."

She laughed when she saw my confusion.

"He wasn't your bloody uncle, you silly cow. He was your father."

It felt like I'd been hit by an iron bar. Suddenly, it all made sense. How had I not seen it?

"And now he's gone," she said. "Who do you think paid for this place? Who paid the bills? Who sent you to posh schools? Well, that's all over now."

A second iron bar hit me. My hands dropped to the sofa to prevent me from swaying. My world was crashing around my ears and she was smiling maliciously.

"I was his bit on the side," she drawled. "That's what he called me. It was all right, too, until you came along. You weren't part of the plan; you weren't wanted."

How many more iron bars would whack me today? Redheads have a reputation; largely unwarranted. But I warranted it that day. I slapped my mother across the face; hard. Then again, harder.

I can still see the look on her face now. Shock, disbelief, pain. She broke down and wept. To this day, I've no idea why she was crying. Grief about Allan's death? Fear for her future? Shame for what she'd said? Or the pain from my hand.

I left her there and went to my room. Lying on my bed, my head was bursting. I'd loved Allan, but what now? Now I knew the truth they'd hidden from me for eighteen years. I'd finally found out who my father was a few days after he died. He'd been around all along.

But my mother was right about one thing; the money dried up. Allan's wife knew about us but had never had contact. A solicitor came to see us and after a lot of waffle, the bare facts were clear. We had six months to vacate the house.

Allan had left my mother a relatively small sum of money; she shrieked as she heard the amount. I paid little attention to the news he'd left me something in a trust fund. After he left, we sat there. Mother was inconsolable.

"What am I going to do?" she repeated over and over again.

I didn't know the answer. She hadn't worked since I'd been born and had few skills. I must admit, her future was not in the forefront of my mind. I was thinking about what I was going to do.

Chapter 2 - Party Girl

We weren't invited to Allan's funeral. I was glad. Mother would have made a spectacle of herself, and my feelings for Allan had changed. Why had he denied me? Why had they not told me the truth? His wife knew we existed, so why all the secrecy?

I had to get out of the house. Mum was drunk all the time and wallowing in self-pity. I soon realised it wasn't grief at Allan's death, I don't think she ever loved him. She'd loved his money. It had kept her for at least eighteen years. It was ironic she regretted having me. I suspect that if it hadn't been for me, and some semblance of honour in Allan, he would have dumped her years ago for a younger mistress. It was my arrival that guaranteed her longevity.

I didn't know where to go. I had a few friends who lived in London, but we weren't close enough for me to turn up on their doorsteps with a case. I spent my days wandering around the city. Museums, galleries, anywhere I could spend time for free. Money was a concern. Allan had always given me something when he visited, but only small amounts. I had no income and my mother wasn't exactly generous.

Every night, I returned home to find her surrounded by empty bottles and cigarette packets. The few times I tried to talk to her or help her, I was rebuffed ferociously and soon gave up. I was thinking about the future. When my exam results arrived, they were even better than expected; I could go to university. But did I want to?

I met a couple of friends and asked them if I could unload. I told them most of the story except for my father's identity. They were surprised but told me to go for it. If I didn't go to uni, what would I do? Those three years of studying would give me thinking time and a future. I knew they were right, but I decided to turn down my first choice and stay in London.

When I told mother, she was her usual mocking self and by the time I moved into the university halls, she hadn't made any progress on finding somewhere else to live. When I went to visit her a few weeks later, the house was empty. Fortunately, a neighbour had her new address. A grotty little flat in Hammersmith which stank of alcohol and tobacco. She'd aged years in a few months and wasn't happy to see me. After a few brief words, I left.

I enjoyed the first year at university. I made some good friends and loved the life. Money was always tight, but I took a couple of part-time jobs in the holidays to supplement the grants. In those days, work at university wasn't too onerous. A few lectures and a couple of tutorials a week, some private study time and the rest was yours. I had fun.

I'd discovered sex quite early; initially, on my own. Going to a girl's school was a good education, if a little confusing. We talked about it all the time and did a bit of experimenting. Our knowledge was limited and often wrong, but the will was there.

University was a different world. We were adults and did adult things. I found myself having sex for real. AIDS was prevalent, so we were careful, but it didn't stop us. I was still naïve and looking back it was all ordinary and mundane. A quick fuck, he came and that was it. It was okay, but I hadn't found anyone to show me what I was missing.

I discovered to my surprise that I was attractive to boys. I had grown tall, reaching six feet and I was conscious of it when I met a guy who was shorter than me. Some didn't like it, I guess they may have been intimidated.

But my hair proved a hit. Since I'd come to accept it, it had become something of an obsession. I grew it long, almost to my waist, and I could style it in a dozen different ways. Some guys were drawn to it like moths to a flame. I learnt to tie it up on dates, and slowly undo it all, letting it hang free once we were back in his room or mine. It seemed to turn them on. They loved me letting it fall all over them as we fucked.

I also loved someone playing with it; combing it, running their fingers through it. It became something of a fetish for me. It still is.

Most of my affairs were short; none of them lit my fire, although I wasn't sure what that meant. I made a friend in Carla. She was the same age and shared my sense of humour. We found ourselves going to the same pubs and clubs and ended up spending a lot of our free time together.

"Going out on Friday?" she asked one day.

"I don't think so," I replied. "No money until the next grant cheque."

"What if I take you somewhere that won't cost a penny?"

"Like where?"

"A little party."

Friday evening, I found myself getting ready for a party somewhere. Carla hadn't told me where, but she'd told me to dress up, so I went the whole hog. When she arrived to collect me, she gave me the once over and smiled.

"Gordon will love you," she said.

"Gordon?"

"It's his party."

We took the tube to Sloane Square and walked to a large house in Selwood Terrace. When the door opened, a big guy in a black suit let us in. The house was full of people and the sounds indicated the party was in full swing. Carla headed towards a door set to one side and went through.

"Hi, Gordon," she said.

"Well, well, the beautiful Carla. And who's this?"

"This is Bella."

Gordon looked me over carefully, his eyes taking in everything. He was a man of around fifty; well-groomed and smartly dressed. His face betrayed a sharp intelligence.

"An appropriate name," he said.

I'd heard that line so many times. I suspected Gordon used it ironically, but a lot of younger boys seemed to believe they were the first to think of it.

"Have you told her the setup?" he asked.

"Not yet, but I will."

I didn't like being talked about in my presence. Carla led me through another door into a large room with a few chairs and tables covered in coats and bags.

"Right," Carla said. "It's simple. We're the bait."

I frowned.

"Gordon runs these parties and guys pay a lot of money to attend. He provides lots of beautiful girls."

I didn't like where this was going, and it must have shown on my face.

"Don't worry," she said. "It's not what you think."

"I don't know ..."

"The guys here are looking for some relaxed fun. All you've got to do is be friendly."

She could see my doubts.

"Look, Bella. We go out to a pub or club and end up in bed with some grubby student. It's no different here, except these guys are rich and can be very generous."

"Generous?"

"Yes."

"Really?"

"Yea."

"Have you ...?"

"Yup. I've got one on the go at the moment. Nice guy."

"No!"

"Yea. I meet him once a week. A good meal in a fancy restaurant in exchange for a couple of hours in a hotel."

"Carla!"

"It's so easy, Bella. Candy from babies."

My head was buzzing. Part of me wanted to run, but she was right. The guys I was fucking weren't exactly thrilling. Half of them were instantly forgettable. If there were some nice guys here, what was the harm? She was looking expectantly at me.

"All right," I said. "I'll give it a try."

"Great. Just be picky."

Picky? I was nineteen and my experience of men was limited to other students who knew little more about sex than I did. They may not have been very good, but they had no agenda apart from sex. I was about to enter a whole different world where I felt truly out of my depth.

We checked our appearance in a mirror by another door and Carla led me through, coming out into a large hallway with an elaborate staircase leading upstairs. There were people milling about, chatting, and laughing. Everyone was smartly dressed; the guys in suits and the women in party gear. Lots of big hair; we were still just in the eighties. Carla led me to a bar and ordered some drinks.

"Better than Glitter, isn't it?" she said. Glitter was the nearest club to our flat.

"Yea, it sure is."

In truth, an abandoned abattoir would have been an improvement on Glitter.

"What now?" I asked.

"Just wait," she replied.

We didn't have to wait long. A couple of minutes later, a tall guy approached me and asked if I'd like a drink. When I accepted, he perched on the stool next to me.

"I'm Martin," he said.

"Bella."

"Hi, Bella. I haven't seen you here before."

"This is my first time."

"Ah, I'm lucky then."

"Lucky?"

11

"To get to you first. I think there'll be lots of competition to speak to the owner of such beautiful hair."

Even in my naiveté, I knew a corny chat-up line when I heard one, but he wasn't pushy. He was good looking and friendly, with an easy manner. He stayed for ten minutes or so, then excused himself and wandered off. Turning around, I found Carla had gone. I was on my own.

She was right about one thing. You didn't have to do anything but wait. Over the next hour or so, several guys introduced themselves, bought me a drink and chatted for a few minutes. I felt I was being auditioned; I guess I was. At one point, I needed the loo and asked the barman who pointed me in the right direction.

When I found the door, it was locked, and a passing guest told me to try upstairs. When I reached the landing, I was a bit lost, but another guest gave me directions. I pushed open the door and stopped in my tracks. Not three feet in front of me was an unforgettable tableau. One guy leaning against the sink, his trousers around his ankles and his cock in a girl's mouth. Her dress was over her back and another guy was fucking her. I stammered something and hurriedly reversed. As I shut the door, I heard some laughter and an invitation to join the fun.

Standing in the corridor, I was a bit light-headed. I hadn't been expecting what I'd seen; not in a million years. It wasn't that I was offended, they all seemed to be enjoying themselves. But in the bathroom?

"You alright?" a voice asked.

I turned to see Carla coming along the corridor.

"Uh, yes. I ... think so."

"What's up?"

"Two guys ... and a girl ..."

"They should have locked the door. Come on, there's another loo around the corner."

Thinking back, I find it funny that what surprised Carla was not what they were doing, but that they forgot to lock the door.

"Found anyone nice?" Carla asked.

"I don't know. They all seemed okay."

"Anyone you fancied?"

"Not especially."

"Anyone asked you out?"

"No. You?"

"One or two, but I turned them down."

"Why?"

"Just a feeling."

I suddenly felt out of my depth. A feeling? A feeling for what? As we came down the stairs, I turned to Carla.

"I need to leave," I said.

"If you want. Let's go and see Gordon."

As we headed across the hall, I heard my name. Turning, I saw Martin coming towards us.

"Leaving already?" he asked.

"Yes. It's all a bit much."

"And I was going to come and talk to you again."

"Were you?"

Carla discreetly moved away.

"Yes. But as you're leaving, I won't be able to. How about I buy you dinner one evening?"

I thought quickly. What's the harm?

"That sounds nice."

He pulled a card out of his jacket and wrote the name of a restaurant on the back.

"Friday at seven?" he said, handing me the card before turning and walking away.

"See," Carla said, having sidled up behind me. "He looks nice."

"Mmm."

She led the way back into the room Gordon seemed to use as his office.

"Leaving already?" he said.

"Yes," Carla said. "It's all been a bit much for Bella."

"I hope you'll come again," he said to me.

"I might, I don't know."

"She has got herself a date, though," Carla said. His face brightened.

"That's good. Here you go."

He held out two small envelopes; Carla took hers and I tentatively accepted mine.

"See you both soon," he said, as we made our way through to the door. When we'd walked a little way along the street, I turned to Carla.

"What's in the envelopes?"

"Happy pills."

"What?"

"Happy pills."

"I've never tried them."

When we got home, I did. The only effect I could discern was they kept me awake all night. A bit of a high, but nothing else. Carla, on the other hand, changed remarkably. Giggling, talkative but relaxed. It was funny at first, but as it became clear I wasn't going to sleep, it quickly got boring. Then she fell fast asleep and started snoring. I could have killed her.

Chapter 3 - First Date

Martin watched me as I looked around the restaurant. It was a departure for me, particularly since money had become tight. Even when my father had taken us out, it was always to discreet places. This was an iconic restaurant and it showed.

"Nice, isn't it?" he asked.

"Yes. Sorry, not been here before."

"That's okay. I like it."

I was jumpy. This was my first proper date. I'd been to pubs and clubs with boys, but never anything this formal. As a student, you didn't do formal. I'd dressed as well as I could and Martin had complimented my appearance, but he was a bit of a smoothie. I quite liked it.

He was also very relaxed, and his calmness slowly rubbed off on me. He asked where I came from, about my family, what I wanted to do. I was careful with my answers. My mother was deteriorating. I didn't see her often, and she was worse every time I did.

He told me about himself; something in commodities. I vaguely knew what that meant but wasn't really interested.

"Single?" I asked him.

"Yes, as it happens. Not ready to settle down yet. Just looking for some fun."

I could only take him at his word. Did it matter? Not really. By turning up, I'd accepted how I was going to pay for this meal. I'd thought about that; did it bother me?

No. Since my father's death, life had changed. Money was tight and fun was in short supply. University had brought me into contact with all sorts of people. Many as poor as me, but others who lived a different life. I wanted a taste of it.

He'd been right about the restaurant, it was good. The food was the best I'd eaten in a long time, and the wine flowed. He was charming and thoughtful, listening to me and not always talking about himself. After we'd finished eating, I wondered what happened next. This was all new for me and he knew it.

"What are you thinking?" he asked during a lull in the conversation.

I didn't know what to say. Should I skate the issue or be blunt?

"I'm not sure what happens now," I replied.

"Whatever you want," he said.

"What do you want?" I asked him.

He swirled the wine in his glass and looked me in the eye. "You."

I felt myself blush, no one had been so direct. The boys I'd been to bed with had been as nervous as me and it had all been mumbling and fumbling. This was refreshing.

"Okay," I replied.

"Just like that?"

"What else should I say?"

He paid the bill and when we left the restaurant, he put his arm around me, and we walked a couple of streets to a hotel. Nothing exceptional, but smart enough. By the time we got to the room, I was in two minds. Part of me was excited. I was still naïve. I'd never had a lover who was so self-assured, and I wondered if that would make a difference; if it would be better than my brief experiences so far. The other part of me wanted to run.

He went to the bathroom, and without thinking, I stripped. My experiences to date hadn't lasted long. We'd got naked and I'd laid there while the guy fucked me. That was all I knew. When he came out of the bathroom, he saw me lying on the bed and smiled.

"You don't mess about, do you?" he said.

"It's what you want, isn't it?"

"Yes, but there's plenty of time."

"For what?"

He sat on the bed.

"You're not a virgin, are you?"

"No."

"Much experience?"

"Not really."

"Have you enjoyed it?"

I thought for a moment.

"Not much so far."

"Let's see if we can change that. Turn over."

I rolled onto my front, not knowing what to expect. His hand brushed my back and trailed up and down my spine. His other hand lifted my hair, which I'd tied in a loose ponytail. He undid the ties and laid it over my shoulders onto the pillow beside me.

"You're tense," he said.

My body was a bundle of tight muscles, my arms rigid by my side. He stood and I turned my head to watch him shed his clothes. He was fit and toned, but I was surprised to see his cock still flaccid. My previous lovers had all been desperate by this stage.

He got back on the bed and knelt by my side. Placing his hands on my back his fingers lightly brushed my skin from neck to the base of my spine. I was confused; I'd expected him to fuck me for a few minutes and that would be that. But his touch was delicate, it was warming me. My shoulders dropped to the bed, relaxing.

He moved and straddled my thighs; his cock resting on my bum. Easing my arms away from my side, he resumed his stroking, his hands now free to wander along my flanks. I started to enjoy this attention and moved my arms to rest my head on them.

He increased the pressure and ran his hands up and down my back and I heard myself groan as he did so. He shuffled down my legs and let his hands run over my bum, stretching, and caressing it. Moving up again, he laid over me, and I felt his weight on me. A whisper in my ear surprised me.

"Feeling calmer?"

"Yes."

"Good."

I shivered as he kissed my neck and kept on kissing it, moving every time. Gradually moving down my back and reaching my bum. I gave a little shriek as he playfully bit a cheek and chuckled at my response. His kissing continued down one leg, all the way to my feet.

My body felt different somehow. I knew I was enjoying his attention. I'd given myself orgasms but hadn't had one with a guy yet. What little I knew seemed to tell me this wasn't unusual, but I was keenly aware of my body now. It was warm, relaxed and my groin was definitely heating up. When he got me to turn over, my nipples were erect as well.

He climbed over me and gave me a kiss; our first kiss. Gentle and delicate; not the combative tongue-fencing I'd experienced up to now. He carried the kisses on, down my neck to my breasts, circling them, cupping them until he reached a nipple. I groaned as his lips sucked it, surprised by my sensitivity. He flicked it with his tongue a few times before moving to the other.

Then he slid down my body, laying delicate kisses all over my tummy. I felt previously unknown muscles twitch in response. I was conscious of where he was going. His kisses reached my pubic hair and still he carried on. I raised my head to look.

"Just relax," he said, and I let my head drop on the pillow. My legs were still together, and he kissed down one thigh, and up the other. When he reached my bush again, I let him open my legs and his kisses moved to the inside of my thighs. This was all new to me; I knew about oral sex, but it was a bit of a mystery.

The mystery began to be solved as his mouth landed over my sex, making me gasp. I felt his tongue pushing into me, as he sucked me towards him. My hips squirmed with pleasure as he found sensitive spots I didn't know I had. He released me and my groin relaxed, only to jump again as his mouth surrounded my clit.

I bit my lip as he rolled it from side to side, slowly pushing the hood until his tongue pressed down firmly and lapped at it. I knew I was going to have an orgasm; so did he. He set an even rhythm and my hips rose until I let out a gasp and came, a series of spasms followed by a couple of random twitches.

He laid his head on my thigh and when I finally looked at him, he was watching me, smiling. I smiled back and reached down to stroke his hair.

"More relaxed now?" he asked.

"Yes, much more."

"Good."

He got to his knees and I saw he was stiff now. He reached over to the bedside cabinet, picked up a condom, undid the packet and rolled it on. Picking up a pillow, he placed it under my bum and edged himself between my legs. I felt the head nudge into place, then slowly slide into me, much more easily than it had in my earlier adventures.

He leaned over me and bent to kiss me. I surprised myself with my fervent response, pulling him onto me and gasping as his weight drove his cock deeper inside me. He was in need now and began to fuck me, and I found myself opening my legs wider to encourage him.

He switched his action, sliding up and down, his pelvic bone rubbing across my clit and I was amazed to find myself near orgasm again. As I came, he gave a loud grunt and I felt him jerk inside me; his movement slowing as he completed his climax before dropping on me, breathing heavily.

19

He lifted off to allow him to remove his sheathed cock, before settling on me again and I put my arms around him. I was glowing; it was the best sex I'd ever had. I'd actually enjoyed it. If sex could be like this, I wanted more. I got it sooner than I expected.

After he cleaned up, we lay on the bed and I told him the entire history of my sex life; it didn't take long. He smiled and offered me a deal. He'd already told me he wasn't looking for anything permanent, I hadn't expected it. But he'd take me out once a week and teach me whatever I wanted to learn. When he'd shown me everything he knew, we'd part.

I readily agreed and, to my surprise, we sealed the deal by fucking again, this time with him taking me on all fours. This was something I'd only done a couple of times and briefly at that, with my inexperienced lovers. But this time, his fingers made sure I had another orgasm before he grabbed my hips and fucked me hard and deep, bringing himself to another climax.

Martin and I saw each other for three months. Every week, we went on a date; a restaurant, a bar, a couple of concerts. Then a few hours in a hotel, occasionally the whole night. Even though I say so myself, I was a quick learner; but he was a good teacher. He'd passed on all he knew within two months, but we kept going because we enjoyed each other. And practice makes perfect.

He also taught me to love myself. As a teenager, I had grown tall and gangly and I tended to slouch in an effort to hide my height. But I'd filled out and he encouraged me to be proud of my size and shape. It was possibly the most important lesson he taught me.

When we parted, he gave me a beautiful pair of earrings. He had given me little gifts throughout, as well as money to get some underwear or a dress. He loved stylish underwear, and I quickly discovered I did too. It made me feel confident and sexy. Why, I've never been able to explain, but it became a passion that has stayed with me ever since.

Chapter 4 - Catfight

At the end of the first year of university, Carla and I rented a flat with a couple of other girls. It was big but dilapidated. One bathroom for four girls would prove a problem and it was freezing in winter, but it gave us freedom.

I opened the flat door one morning to find a policeman, looking for me. I wasn't surprised by his message. My mother had been found dead in her flat and I had to go and identify her. I only just recognised her; she was almost skeletal.

Then I had to clear out her flat and deal with her belongings. There weren't many by now, but the flat was in a disgusting state. Carla was a gem; she helped me with everything. Even the cleaning, which wasn't a pleasant job at all. I kept virtually nothing of my mother's. She'd sold anything of value and the rest went to the tip. I packed up all her papers and photographs and took them home.

Her funeral was a sorry affair. A few people I didn't know who turned out to be friends she'd made in the last couple of years; most of them seemed to be fellow alcoholics and dropouts. They sloped off after the brief ceremony, muttering to themselves when they found out I hadn't organised any refreshments.

One evening after I settled everything, I took a deep breath and went through her papers. Most of it went straight in the bin, but two things were of interest. One was details of the trust fund my father had set up for me. I'd forgotten about it after he died. It didn't detail the amounts but did say there would be a small payment when I was twenty-one, with the rest being paid when I reached twenty-five, or earlier if I got married.

The other was a restraining order, preventing my mother making any contact with my father's wife or family. I could only guess what had happened, but I was fairly sure she tried to get money out of them. It would have been typical of her. I wrote them a short letter, informing them of my mother's death, apologising for her behaviour and assuring them I would not be the cause of any further trouble. I told them they didn't need to reply, but I did get a little note from his son, thanking me for informing them and wishing me well in the future. We had no further contact.

As I was nearing my twenty-first birthday, I approached the solicitor about the first part of the settlement. When it arrived, I got a shock. Five thousand pounds. I'd never had so much money.

Carla may have been my best friend but our outlook on life was quite different. I was still a little naïve, though Martin had helped me broaden my horizons. I still considered things carefully before committing myself. Carla was the opposite; try anything once, possibly two or three times. When I got the money, we were still on summer break, so I took her on holiday to Spain for a couple of weeks. We had a grand time, plenty of sun and alcohol. And for Carla, plenty of sex. She had a different guy nearly every night, sometimes with another during the day.

Martin had spoilt me. I wasn't happy with the same old thing all the time. He'd shown me the possibilities and I hadn't found anyone as good. I tried but was disappointed on most occasions.

When we got back, Carla introduced me to a group of her friends. I'd met several of them already, but never been a part of the set. They were mostly wealthy and made me a little uncomfortable. She took me to a party on a riverboat one evening and I realised why Carla was so welcome. She was their supplier.

"Yea," she said. "I get it from someone I know."

"Carla, this could get you into trouble."

"Bella, it's okay."

"But do you deal the hard stuff?"

"Nah, only weed and some pills. If you want harder stuff, try Dave over there."

She pointed to a guy standing slightly apart from everyone else. As I watched, someone went over to him, and they did a furtive exchange in a matter of seconds. So, she was just one of their suppliers.

"Want one?" Carla asked, holding out a joint. I wasn't averse to smoking weed, we did it regularly. I took it and she lit it; we shared it. It calmed me, no great reaction, but I became mellow and slightly giggly. By the end of the evening, we were both high. How we found our way home, I have no idea.

We went to another party the following week, and it became a regular event; lots of booze, plenty of drugs and people wandering off somewhere private for a quickie. I was still careful, happy with a joint and one or two pills. The harder stuff scared me. Not Carla. I found her at one party, snorting coke from a bar with another girl I didn't know.

"Want some?" she asked.

"No thanks," I said. "Not my scene."

"Come on," the other girl said. "Give it a go. Feels great."

"Yea," Carla said. "This is Fran, by the way."

I'd noticed Fran. She was a stunning blonde, always immaculately dressed.

"Hi, Fran. Bella."

Within ten minutes, they were both talking ten to the dozen. I couldn't keep up. But within half an hour, they needed more and started laying them out.

"Bella, Bella," Fran said. "Try a line."

I took the step, coughing and half-choking after I'd snorted it. Very quickly feeling the effects. I'd never experienced anything like it; confidence, control, an aura of invincibility. But it didn't last long before I needed another.

"Whoa," Carla said. "Slow down. Take a break. You're not used to it."

I needed the loo anyway and wandered off to find it. As I walked, I was with it enough to think about the effect coke was having on me. I didn't feel high as I did on ecstasy or after a strong joint. It was more an overwhelming feeling of confidence. I could have done anything at that moment.

I turned a corner and nearly bumped into a guy I'd noticed before; tall, dark, and handsome. Something of a cliché, but in my state, very alluring. Because I'd noticed one other effect; I was feeling aroused. I needed sex.

"Oh, sorry," he said.

"That's okay," I said. "I need something."

He smiled.

"Really?"

"Yea."

"What?"

"Well, the loo, to start with."

"It's down here."

He led me to a corridor and pointed to a door.

"Thanks," I said, opening it and going in.

When I came out, he was standing at an open door a few yards away, holding a little bag of white powder, smiling. I didn't need a second invitation and followed him into a small bedroom. We were soon snorting a line from the table. We sat for a few minutes, both of us knowing exactly what was going to happen.

He stood and held out a hand. As soon as I grabbed it, he spun me around and pushed me onto the bed. I got on my hands and knees and saw him rolling a condom on his cock. He stood behind me, lifted my dress, and pulled my knickers to one side.

I let out a giggling groan as he pushed into me. I'd never wanted to be fucked so badly. He started to drive in and out, and almost immediately, my head started to swim. I felt an orgasm coming, but when it came, it was different. No great explosion, merely a mild high and a heat in my groin. Not my usual climax.

But I didn't care; he was still fucking me, and I waited for something better. Then the door opened.

"You bastard." A woman's voice. His action stopped and I turned to see Fran standing in the doorway. She came towards us and slapped him across the face. His cock slid out of me, and I collapsed onto the bed.

"What's going on?" she said.

I giggled and she glared at me.

"Honey," he stammered. "I- "

She slapped him again and when I went to stand up, she slapped me. I'd never been slapped before and my drug-induced confidence took over. I hurled myself at her, taking her by surprise. We fell into a heap on the floor and started hitting each other; flat hands, nails, fists. Lots of screams.

People appeared and pulled us apart, taking us to different rooms.

"Well," Carla said when she arrived. "You're a bit of a mess."

When I looked in the mirror, I saw she was right. I had a few streaks of blood on my face and a couple of nail scratches, and the back of my head hurt. Carla gently pulled my hair apart.

"We need to go to the nearest hospital," she said.

"What?"

"There's a deep gash here, it'll need stitches."

She gave me a towel to press on the wound and with me grumbling and muttering, led me out of the room. Gathering our things, she called a taxi and we headed to the hospital. It was Friday night and the place was packed.

"Sorry," I said. The coke was wearing off, my head was beginning to hurt, and I felt a fool.

"Not sure I'm letting you have any more," she replied.

I froze as Fran was brought in by another girl, a towel over her face, covered in a lot of blood. We looked at each other and after they registered, they sat at the opposite end of the waiting room. I was called into triage. Nothing but cuts and bruises on my face, but Carla had been right. The wound on my head would need a few stitches.

Fran was treated before me and I wondered why. After an hour or so, I found out. I was called through and placed in the same holding area as her, a couple of chairs apart. The effects of the coke had largely worn off and we were now at the grudging acceptance phase. Her face was a mess; blood caked all over it, particularly her nose.

"I ... I'm sorry," I mumbled.

"Yea," she said, "me too. Bastard." I frowned. "Not you, Gavin." A macabre grin appeared on her bloodied face. "I thought I'd hooked him."

"Was that his name?" I said, and she burst out laughing.

"You didn't hang around. Didn't even ask his name."

"I'm not usually like that."

She swapped chairs to sit beside me.

"It's the coke," she whispered. "Makes me horny as hell."

"Ah."

We sat silent for a few moments.

"What's your damage?" she asked.

"Nothing much on my face, but a big gash on the back of my head. I've no idea how that happened."

"You hit the edge of the door. Apparently, you left a few bits of skin and hair behind."

It made sense now.

"And you?" I asked.

"Broken nose."

I flinched.

"I guess that must have been me."

"Probably," she said. "I hope it's not bent, that's all. I'm not picking a fight with you again."

"I'm so sorry. I've never hit anyone in my life."

26

She shrugged.

"Forget it."

"So, is Gavin ..."

"Not anymore. Quite funny really."

"What is?"

"He never got to come."

I'd forgotten that and it made me smile, too. They called me to a cubicle and a nurse shaved away a small area of hair and stitched me up. She warned me the hair might not grow back properly over the wound.

"But you've got so much beautiful hair, you'll easily be able to cover it."

She proved to be right on both counts. She checked the other scrapes and bruises, but there was nothing a good wash and a few days recovery wouldn't mend. As I walked along the corridor, I passed the cubicle where Fran was lying on the bed.

"How are you doing?" I asked.

"It's broken but they reckon it's not out of shape. Apparently, I'm going to swell up like a balloon."

"Oh."

"If it's kinked, I've got to come back for them to straighten it."

A nurse appeared.

"Is this your friend?" she asked.

"No," Fran replied. "This is the fiend who broke it."

The nurse looked worried and looked at my injuries.

"Do I need to have her removed?"

"No, we've made up."

The nurse shook her head.

"Well," she said. "You can go now. Come back if you get a lot of bleeding, or if it's out of shape when the swelling goes down."

We walked out to the waiting area together, much to the surprise of Carla and Fran's friend, who were now sitting together and chatting.

"Are you two okay?" Carla asked nervously.

"Yea," Fran replied. "We're arranging round two."
In truth, we'd both found a soulmate.

Chapter 5 - Selling Myself

Fran's friend left us to go back to the party, but we weren't feeling, or looking, up to it. Although the coke's effect had largely worn off, we were all wide awake, and we invited Fran to come home with us. Carla looked around the flat for alcohol; there wasn't much. But she always had a good supply of weed and a variety of pills. Fran was in pain, and a joint or two seemed to help. Strangely, my head was just a dull ache.

"You two students?" Fran asked. We told her a bit about our lives.

"You?" Carla asked.

"Media studies. Boring as hell, but it gets me a grant."

She was a couple of years older than Carla and me, and it showed. Her view of the world was more mature and cynical than ours.

"Where are you from?" I asked her.

"Newcastle."

"Why come down here?"

"I wanted to get away. My family are dirt poor. I grew up on a run-down council estate, Dad always in and out of work. My brothers were in trouble when they were twelve or thirteen."

"How did you escape that?"

"A teacher helped me after school and made me believe I could do better. I went to college and got good enough results to go to uni. My family always laughed at me, so I decided to leave them behind. London seemed to be ideal."

"Is it?"

She gave a hollow laugh.

"Well, it's full of possibilities."

She told us how she'd come with the best of intentions; in her first year, she studied hard and kept her nose clean. But by the second year, she saw others doing things differently.

"I wasn't able to do much. No money. There's so much to do here, but you need cash to do it."

"We know that feeling, don't we?" Carla said.

"So, I started to mingle with my betters; the type who were at the party. They've always got money."

"But how do you get it?"

She looked at me as if I was an idiot.

"Sex," she said.

Carla and I looked at each other, very aware of our brief forays into Gordon's world and intrigued by Fran's answer.

"Sex?"

"Yea. Men are idiots; as are some women."

She softened when she saw our interest.

"Oh, come on, you can't be that naïve. You were at those parties, and I'm guessing neither of you are millionaire's daughters. Why were you there?"

We told her, and about Gordon and his parties.

"We're all in the same business," she said with a grin.

"It's just a bit of fun," I said, defensively. I was still uncomfortable with the idea of selling myself.

"It is," Fran said. "But why not profit from it, as well?"

She told us how she operated. Worked her way into a promising group and homed in on a likely target.

"I don't lie; I tell them I expect something in return, but it doesn't usually stop them. I've had a few lucrative arrangements so far."

"And Gavin was your next target," I said.

"Yes, but there'll be plenty of others."

Fran slept on the couch and when we got up in the morning, we agreed to meet again when her face had healed. It took three weeks; she never let me forget it.

We were all single and free and when we met again, we decided to give Gordon a visit. He was delighted to see us and welcomed Fran. The party was just the same. Martin was there and gave me a hug and a kiss, but we were in each other's past now. Time to look to the future.

Over the next few months, we all found a guy or two, but none of them led to anything meaningful. We'd stopped going out with the other group; after our catfight, we knew we wouldn't be welcome. The money I'd had from the trust fund was nearly gone and I had nothing to show for it. Just regular evenings fuelled by drugs and alcohol. But it was fun, and I didn't want it to stop. We had to find a solution and it was Gordon who provided it.

We were leaving one of his parties, none of us having been successful.

"Don't worry, girls. There's always next week."

"It's not fun anymore," Carla said.

"What's up, babe?"

"We're skint, Gordon."

He looked at each of us in turn, weighing us up.

"What are you prepared to do?" he asked, leaning back in his seat. We looked at each other.

"What do you mean?" Fran said.

"These aren't the only parties I'm involved with," he replied.

"Go on."

"I provide beautiful women for private parties, but they're a bit different."

"Meaning?" Fran had appointed herself our spokesperson; I wasn't complaining.

"You'd have to put out."

"What's it worth?"

I gasped at her casual acceptance of the idea.

"Depends," he replied. "Not less than three hundred each."

At that, I gasped again.

"Tell us more," she said. As he gave us the details, I could hardly believe my ears. Was I really contemplating this?

"We'll let you know, Gordon," Fran said when he'd finished.

As we left the house, nothing was said; each of us with our own thoughts. Fran led us to a nearby wine bar and we ordered some drinks and a few snacks. The silence continued as we picked at them.

"Well?" Fran finally asked.

"I don't know," Carla said. "It's a big step."

"Oh, come on," Fran replied. "We've all been looking for some guy to give us a free meal in return for sex. How is this different? And here, the money's guaranteed."

She had a point.

"But there'd be a lot of sex, from what Gordon said," Carla replied. "I've never had more than one guy in a day."

"Yes, you have," I said. "On holiday, remember?"

She grinned.

"Oh, yea."

We thought about it for a week, a week in which my money finally ran out. That made the decision for us. We went to see Gordon.

We were on the DLR heading to Docklands, all dressed up and definitely somewhere to go. I was shaking; a gentle tremor, but it was there, even after two joints. Fran seemed calm; she'd already assumed the leadership role in the group. Nothing seemed to faze her, and her confidence was catching. Walking from the station to the address, we said little and when Fran rang the buzzer, the reality of the situation hit me. My legs nearly buckled.

The lift took us to the fifteenth floor and when it opened, we found ourselves looking at a familiar face. One of the doormen from the Selwood Terrace house.

"Ladies," he said, and we followed him along the corridor. Gordon had told us he always had one of his people at these events. It made me feel more comfortable.

He led us to one of the apartments and opened the door. We followed him in, and he pointed out the bathroom, before leading us through to the main reception area. There was some music in the background and the gentle hum of conversation, which died as we entered.

A quick look around revealed six or seven men, who had already been joined by three girls. One I recognised from Selwood Terrace, but the others I didn't know. The conversation restarted as one of the guys came over and welcomed us; his party, I guess. He took us to the bar.

"Help yourselves, girls. Whatever, whenever."

It was well stocked with alcohol, and an array of drug paraphernalia littered one end. Carla immediately cut three lines of coke. Her outer confidence was only skin deep, as was mine and we took a line each. I felt the effects quickly, that growth in confidence which I needed.

Turning to the room, we looked around.

"Right," Fran said. "Pick a spare man each."

She walked towards a guy sitting on his own, perched herself on the arm of his chair and started talking. I hoped I could be as smooth. I saw a guy standing by the window, sipping a drink, and watching proceedings. I headed over to him.

"Hi," I said, in a voice so forced, even I didn't recognise it.

"Hello, red," he said. I'd tied my hair in a tight plait, but I could never hide the colour. Not that I wanted to. The coke had given me courage and I started talking. I have no idea what about and he listened with an amused air, adding the occasional brief comment. When he emptied his glass, I offered to get him a refill and headed to the bar.

On my return, I was taken aback when I looked over to the other side of the room. One of the girls was on the floor between a guy's legs, sucking his cock. He'd already pulled her dress over her bum and was squeezing it. The man next to him had another girl on his lap, his hand between her legs, hidden by her dress. The party had started.

I gave my man his drink and stood uneasily next to him. Things moved quickly. The girl on the floor lifted her dress off and went back to work. The lap girl did the same, allowing a better view of the actions of the man's hand.

We were under strict instructions that underwear mattered here. We were all wearing stockings, with a variety of other pieces. Teddies, lace, silk. I loved it, my passion for expensive lingerie already evident. I jumped as a hand gently squeezed my bum, followed by a gentle chuckle.

"Is this your first time?" he said.

I turned to him.

"Is it that obvious?"

"You know what you've let yourself in for?"

"Oh, yes. I'm not that naïve. Just a bit nervous."

"We'll soon cure that."

He lifted the hem of my dress and put his hand under it, sliding it up my stockings until it reached my bare thigh. I straightened as it continued upwards, ending on my bare bum. He ran it over both cheeks, then traced his fingers back again. I heard a squeal from somewhere in the room and turned to see Fran, now down to her underwear, laying across a guy's lap, his hand between her open legs. Her face told me she wasn't unhappy.

My guy lifted the hem of my dress higher and I took his hint, lifting it over my head. He turned me around and pulled me towards him, my back to him, his arm around my tummy. I surveyed the room.

What I saw was an orgy. The girl was still sucking her guy, the man next to him was now mostly naked and his girl was astride him, sliding up and down on his cock. Fran was still being fingered by her partner. Another girl was on her knees in front of two men, a cock in both hands. And Carla? She was back at the bar with her man, both nearly naked, both snorting a line or two.

My guy pulled me back onto him and his cock pushed into me. His hand left my tummy and headed between my legs and I realised I wanted it. It reached my thong and pushed it aside before his fingers slid over my pussy and pushed into me. I groaned and spread my legs.

Looking over to the bar, I saw Carla bent over one of the stools, her guy fucking her from behind. He wasn't holding back, and I wondered how long she'd be able to hold the precarious position. But I was brought back to my own situation when my guy moved me forward and pushed me over the back of a sofa. I looked around to see him roll a condom on and felt him pull my thong aside and slide his cock in.

I grabbed the arm of the sofa as he fucked me, hoping I'd get the release I needed. As I built to my orgasm, my head jerked back as he pulled my plait. Pulling it firmly, he fucked me hard, slamming into me. I came powerfully, my body dropping onto the upholstery.

He was still fucking me as my climax subsided and opening my eyes, I could see a girl being fucked by two guys, one deep in her pussy, the other enjoying her mouth. It was exciting, a new experience.

I heard a loud groan and felt his movements change as he came, a few hard thrusts pushing deep into me. He gave my ass a slap as he pulled out and held out his hand to help me up.

"Thank you, red. See, it's easy."

He headed off to the bathroom and I went over to join Carla who was still by the bar, but minus her partner.

Chapter 6 - A New Feeling

Round one was nearly over. The only remaining action was the two guys fucking the one girl. As we poured a drink and watched, the guy fucking her came and the other pulled out of her mouth and wanked himself over her face. As she went to clean up, Carla cut some more lines and Fran came over with one of the other girls who she introduced as Mel, telling us the other two were Georgia and Rosie.

Mel grabbed a drink, popped a couple of pills, and left us.

"Well?" Fran asked.

"Okay so far," I replied.

"Yea," Carla said. "Easy enough. Gotta feel sorry for the bouncer."

The security guy had been sitting quietly on a chair in the corner, with a good view of the room.

"If Gordon follows the usual rule, he's gay."

"Really?"

"Yea. If he's not interested, he won't be distracted."

"Makes sense," Carla said.

"Come on, we're paid to entertain the guys, not chat amongst ourselves."

We wandered over to the sofas and attached ourselves to any spare man. They were all naked now, and the girls were left in suspender belts or teddies and stockings. I perched on an arm next to one of the men who'd shared the girl. He wasted no time in pulling me onto him and I landed half on him and half on his neighbour, who already had Mel sitting astride one of his thighs.

I was feeling mellow after another couple of lines of coke. I was ready for just about anything. The next half an hour flew by. Nothing much happened, except the men talking, almost ignoring the naked women all around them. Almost. Hands were exploring skin, crevices, nipples, hair. Gently, almost as an afterthought, but it wasn't unpleasant.

"Who's going to give us a show?" someone said. I didn't know what he meant, but when Mel and Georgia got up and went into the space between the sofas, I understood. The next twenty minutes were to change my life.

The girls knew what was expected of them and did it well enough. Kneeling on the floor, they put their arms around each other and brought their lips together, kissing gently. They let their hands run over each other, through their hair, slowly caressing.

Mel moved down Georgia's body, reaching her breasts and sucking and kissing her nipples. She responded by pulling Mel tighter to her. She was clearly enjoying it, slowly leaning backwards, and laying on the floor, with Mel leaning over her, now kissing her way down Georgia's belly.

I found myself watching intently. I'd had a couple of crushes on girls at school, even had a couple of fingering bouts, but I'd never had sex with a girl. But watching this was affecting me. I was turned on and so was the guy I was sitting on. His cock was stiffening under my bum and the combination was thrilling.

Mel had taken a position between Georgia's legs and was kissing her pussy, using her fingers to open her up and her tongue to slide over the exposed flesh. I wasn't sure if the moans were real, or to please the audience, but she seemed happy enough, guiding Mel's head.

Mel sucked Georgia's clit and the response told me the reactions were real enough. Her body slowly tensed as she approached orgasm, but Mel stopped and her partner dropped, frustrated. Mel smiled and quickly moved around, laying on top, end to end. I lost sight of Georgia's pussy as Mel went down on her again. But I could see Georgia's face, as she lifted slightly to allow her tongue to reach Mel's sex.

I twitched as my guy's hand reached between my legs and roughly rubbed my pussy. I was turned on far more than I had been earlier and reacted to his touch. He pushed me forward, and I looked back to see him roll a condom on. Lifting myself, I grabbed his cock and lowered myself onto him.

I welcomed the feeling of his heat in me, and although his touch was far from delicate, I knew I was heading for my climax. I concentrated on the view. Georgia was pulling Mel onto her and using her tongue to lap up and down the flesh exposed by her fingers.

Georgia groaned as Mel brought her to orgasm and mine followed moments later. Coke gave me confidence and made me horny, but the downside was that my orgasms were diminished. Still enjoyable, but something of a disappointment.

As Georgia's climax dropped, she set to work on Mel but didn't get the chance to finish her. One of the guys knelt behind her and slid his cock into her. He stayed still, letting Georgia use her tongue, just gently rocking. Mel was getting close now, and as she came, the guy couldn't resist. He started to fuck her while another guy knelt in front of her and she took him in her mouth.

My guy now wanted some action and I rode him slowly, his hands groping my breasts. The man next to us was watching, massaging his hard cock and I gave a little squeal as my guy turned us on our side, my head landing on our neighbour's lap.

Lifting myself, I grabbed his cock and took it in my mouth, sliding my lips up and down his erection as the other guy fucked me. I knew he wasn't going to last long and with a few short grunts, I felt him spasm inside me, stop his thrusting and pull out.

My neighbour lifted my head off his cock, reached to the table behind him and rolled a condom on. I straddled him and impaled myself on him. He put his hands on my bum and let me control the action. Within a few minutes, I was heading for another climax and he let me take it, only assuming control when I'd peaked.

He squeezed my cheeks and lifted me; I took the hint and began to ride him hard. A couple of minutes later, he came, grunting and grimacing as he did so. I settled on him, but he lifted me off, his cock dropping out, before pushing me away.

I twisted off him and sat between the two men who had just fucked me; neither said a word. I had my first flash of the reality of my role; I was there to be used, nothing more.

Mel and Georgia were lying on the floor in a soft cuddle, the two men having finished with them. Their closeness caught my eye and I watched them. They were in a world of their own, slowly caressing each other, with gentle smiles on their faces. It was incredibly erotic; more appealing than the actual sex I'd seen earlier.

Two more men had me that night before the party ended at around one in the morning. Gordon's man got us all taxis and I fell asleep as soon as my head hit the pillow.

"Morning, ladies," Gordon said as we entered his office. Carla and I had met up with Fran to go and get our money. The address seemed simple enough, but it took us a while to find it. Eventually, we located it behind a boarded-up strip club on the edge of Soho.

"Morning, Gordon," Fran replied. "You're well-hidden here."

"I used to run the strip joint, but there's no money in it these days, not here. Soho's becoming trendy and they don't want us around anymore. I hear you all did well."

"Really?"

"Yea. Dave's there for your protection, but also for mine. I don't employ hangers-on."

I'd wondered about that and guessed Dave – now I knew his name – was there to keep an eye on us, in every sense of the phrase. Gordon gave us each an envelope and I went to put it in my bag, but Fran opened hers and counted the notes.

"It's all there, girl," he said. "I might be in a dodgy business, but I play fair. I've added a little bonus, as it was your first time. Don't expect it to become a habit."

"If there is a next time," Fran said.

"Up to you," he replied. "But I can always find work for you if you want it."

We left the office, found a nearby café, and ordered a late breakfast. Carla and I discreetly counted the money; four hundred quid.

"Easy money," Carla said. I had to agree, although I still had some reservations. I hadn't accepted the truth of what I'd done; that would take time. Fran was her usual calculating self.

"Yes," she said, looking at each of us. "Do it again?"

For once, we had a logical discussion, giving our impressions of the night before. It hadn't been that bad. The guys had all been okay, and the bar had been welcome. Dutch courage perhaps, but it had eased our first time. We agreed we would do it again but only together.

It turned out that was a normal precaution which Gordon accommodated. It made the girls feel safer if they were working with people they knew. It also made his job easier, because he had teams to call on, rather than hiring individuals.

We worked another party three weeks later; much the same, but more of us and more men. Mel and Georgia were there, but we didn't know the other girls. It was a foreign delegation; I never worked out where from and as they had little English, the evening passed with few words.

Wherever they came from, they were not used to having such willing partners; their inexperience showed and was comical at times. They also loved the alcohol and drugs available and consumed far more than we did. The result was they weren't up to much after the first hour or so, and we spent most of the evening keeping them company rather than anything else.

We wondered if Gordon would get funny about the lack of action and were surprised when he passed on a large bonus. How much he kept himself, we didn't ask.

"I don't care if they talk to you about tractors all evening," he said. "As long as they're happy, you've done well." We didn't complain.

We ended up working twice a month or so and most of my reservations vanished. My only responsibility was to myself and the others felt the same. We were making easy money which allowed us to enjoy the rest of our time.

I did have one thing on my mind. I kept thinking of the impact Mel and Georgia's little show had had on me. We'd found out they were a couple and they got extra for their little shows. But it wasn't the money I was thinking about. Watching them had awoken something in me. It had been intensely erotic, even in the banal setting, and seeing them afterwards, so close, so in tune, had been strangely beautiful.

I enjoyed sex with men. Even at the parties, I got pleasure. I took confidence from Fran and slowly took control of situations. They may be paying me, but it was normally easy to lead the men in the direction you wanted. I took more care of what I wore and made much more of my hair. It attracted attention and made me highly visible. I always worried about the downside, that one of the men would recognise me somewhere else, but hoped they wanted to keep their escapades as private as I did.

But I found myself masturbating to thoughts of women. Not the frantic action, the urgent frigging. But the gentle, soft touching and caressing. I was twenty-two and had never fallen in love with anyone. I wasn't the sentimental kind, but it did feel a little odd. Perhaps I was looking in the wrong place.

Before I worked out where to look, the reality of life intervened again.

Chapter 7 - Dangerous Habits

The university found out about our extra-curricular activities and they didn't like them. We all got letters informing us we were no longer students; unacceptable behaviour. We never discovered how they found out, but after a lot of discussion, we decided not to contest the decision. It would have made everything too public.

Carla and Fran seemed to accept the change in our status easily, but I went through a period of introspection. This hadn't been a part of the plan, such as it was. I'd only gone to university because I had nothing better to do, but I'd thrown myself into it. Now I wouldn't get my degree and whatever opportunities that would bring. I had to change my goals.

We came up with a plan. We went to see Gordon, who told us he saw no problem in providing us with work for the foreseeable future. We all had some money behind us now, so we rented a comfortable three-bedroom flat in Southwark and moved in together.

Working two or three times a month paid far more than a regular nine-to-five job ever would, and with three of us sharing expenses, life became a lot easier. We had a lot of free time to enjoy ourselves. Too much, perhaps.

Fran and I were occasional drug users. We often smoked joints, but the other stuff tended to be on party nights. It made the whole thing easier. But Carla was a regular user now. Weed, pills and coke; she used them every day, and it was changing her. She was distant at times, uncommunicative.

At one party, she went too far, and became aggressive, challenging all the guys to fuck her. They took up the challenge, and we watched our friend being used by seven men, one after the other. It was the first time I felt a touch of fear. The men's lust was up. There were six other girls in the room, but they ignored us and queued for this drugged up girl who'd taunted them.

Gordon wasn't happy and he refused to give Carla work for a month.

"I don't care what you use," he said. "But when you're working for me you stay grounded enough to know what you're doing. You're supposed to have class; street hookers I don't do."

Fran and I went to the next couple of parties without her. We knew most of the other girls by now, so felt safe. At the second party, another couple of girls we didn't know put on a show and my reaction was the same. A guy was fucking me, but I was oblivious to him; my whole being focused on watching them.

When we got home, there was a note from Carla. She'd gone away for a while to clean up and would be back soon. It worried us, we had no way of knowing where she was and no way of contacting her.

"She'll be all right," Fran said.

"I hope so."

"She's not in too deep."

"Yet."

As always after a party, we couldn't sleep. The mixture of drugs and alcohol kept us awake most of the night. We showered as soon as we got home, then sat around in dressing gowns. We talked about anything and everything, often beginning with scathing reviews of the men we'd serviced that night.

"Did you have the little chubby bloke with the combover?" Fran asked.

"Yes, but I hardly noticed."

"I know, he lasted about thirty seconds."

"And was so pleased with himself."

My view of men was being tarnished by the work. They were numbers; some were memorable, but mainly for all the wrong reasons. Some were remembered for their lack of stamina, others for their weird cocks. Some for their ridiculous chat-up lines, hardly needed under the circumstances. The occasional guy stood out as wanting us to enjoy it as well, but they were few and far between.

We were meat. We turned up, they pawed us, groped us, and fucked us. No real human contact was made. We left and got paid. It became routine and I gradually pushed the whole thing into one corner of my mind. It only came out on party days. Just occasionally, it appeared at other times and made me uneasy.

"Those two new girls were good," Fran said.

"Yes," I replied, the memory of their performance still in my mind.

"Interested?" she asked, a questioning expression on her face.

"What do you mean?"

"Come on, Bella. You know exactly what I mean."

"I'm not sure. I guess I'd do it. We've fucked enough guys, what difference would a girl make?"

"You've never had a girl?"

Her surprise was evident in her voice; it made me blush.

"No."

She came towards me and sat close, almost on me, and her arm went around my shoulders and she stroked my hair.

"Want to try?" she asked.

This sudden change took me by surprise, and I was flustered. I was interested, more than she knew, but I hadn't expected it to come this way. I liked Fran a lot, and we got on well. Her body attracted attention too, we'd seen enough of each other. As I thought it through, her hand slid into my dressing gown and brushed my skin.

It was enough. Her touch made me shiver and as I turned to her, she put her lips to mine and kissed me. I let my desire and curiosity take over and responded. Her hand surrounded my breast and began to gently massage it, my nipple already hard. Our kiss went on and on, and my body warmed to this new experience.

She undid the cord on my gown and opened it, exposing my naked form. Her head dipped and she kissed my neck, planting delicate kisses all over it, her hand resting on my hip. I let my head fall back onto the top of the sofa. Her hand strayed over my tummy and up to my breasts, where it cupped one and her mouth moved to cover a nipple.

I gave a little moan as she flicked it with her tongue before repeating the move on my other breast. She came up to kiss me again and smiled when I responded. Standing, she shed her gown, and I lifted off the sofa as she removed mine. When I sat down, she straddled me and leaned against my body, her hands holding my head as she kissed me again. My whole body was waking up, a mellow warmth spreading through me. I wanted this.

Looking into my eyes, she untied my hair, until it was all free and she ran her fingers through it, letting it hang loose. The feel of her skin on mine was glorious and I couldn't resist running my hands up and down her back, finally letting them rest on her bum and stroking it, relishing its softness and warmth.

She leaned forward, bringing her breast close to my mouth and I placed my lips over the nipple, gripping it and squeezing. She gave a little moan and pressed herself forward until I could feel her pubic hair on my tummy. I pulled her towards me, my hands gripping her cheeks tight.

My face was now squashed against her breasts and the feel and smell were intoxicating. She slowly pulled away and ran her hands down my front, over my breasts, my tummy and to my groin, brushing my bush. She stopped before going further and laughed.

"Plenty of time," she whispered and shuffled back, putting her feet on the floor. She opened my legs and knelt between them, reaching over, and kissing my breasts again. Wasting no time, she moved down my tummy until she reached the hairline and I let out a gasp as she pulled a hair or two with her teeth.

Her arms rested on my thighs and her fingers touched me intimately for the first time, slowly stroking the skin around my pussy. My legs opened wider unprompted. She bent down and I felt her tongue run up and down either side of my labia. I wanted to lay back, close my eyes and enjoy it, but the need to watch was overwhelming.

Her tongue moved inward and for the first time, a woman licked my entrance and made me squirm. Her tongue carried on upwards and slid over my clit, making me gasp. She stayed there, encasing the hood with her lips, and using her tongue to flick my bud and I was stunned to find myself coming to a climax. Her touch was perfect, gentle but firm enough. The touch of a woman.

She put her arms under my thighs and maintained her rhythm as my orgasm came. I let my head fall back as it washed over me, strong and delicious. She slowed as it passed, gently kissing my inner thighs. My head came forward and I looked down to see her looking at me, smiling.

I stroked her hair as I recovered, knowing what I wanted to do next. I pulled her to me and kissed her, my scent on her lips. Rolling her over, I slid down her body. I wanted to taste another woman. As I reached her hair, I settled onto my knees and examined her pussy, glistening and pink.

I gently spread her with my fingers, and her scent rose to my nostrils. I took a deep breath, savouring the aroma, before letting my tongue land on her wet folds. Slowly running it up and down, her body gently responding; little contented moans coming from her mouth.

She was as aroused as I had been, making it easy for my novice skills. I let my tongue circle her bud and her response intensified. I enclosed it with my lips and sucked it in and out. Her hand came down and she raked her fingers through my hair. I surprised myself by groaning at her actions and it spurred me on.

I put my hands behind her bum and pulled her towards me, moving my tongue more firmly against her clit. She tensed and dropped as her orgasm came, her body jumping several times as it went through her in waves. She let out a little cry as my last tongue flick proved too much and I stilled, her fingers still crawling through my hair. It was one of the most intimate moments of my life.

I climbed onto the sofa between her legs and leaned against her, her arms coming around me. We didn't move for a long time except for the occasional brush of a finger across skin.

"Good?" Fran asked after kissing my forehead.

"Yes."

"I thought you'd like it."

"Why?"

"I saw you watching Mel and Georgia; the look on your face."

"I hadn't considered it before."

"I've only ever loved women."

I pulled away and turned to her.

"Really?"

"Don't get me wrong, I enjoy fucking men. Well, some of them. They can turn me on, but the emotional connection isn't there. My personal relationships are nearly all female."

I leaned against her again and thought about what she'd said. I understood. Men turned me on too, but it was often impersonal, cold, even. Now, lying against the first woman I'd had sex with, I felt warm and cherished.

We slept together that night, and that's how it stayed. I'd found my first love and we couldn't get enough of each other. I had a lot to learn and Fran was keen to show me.

Carla came home after ten days. She didn't tell us where she'd been and seemed okay, so we didn't push. But we found out soon enough when she started having a regular visitor.

His name was Toby, and Fran recognised him immediately.

"He was at one of the parties," she said, as we snuggled up in bed after another lesson.

"She must be mad," I replied.

Gordon had few rules, but he gave us advice; most of it good, practical stuff. The parties he held at Selwood Terrace were designed for the men to meet girls and make their own arrangements. But the parties we were doing now were quite different. It was all anonymous and fleeting. The men never told us their names and they didn't need to. We were there for the taking. Many girls used false names to protect themselves.

Gordon had told us it wasn't a good idea to arrange to meet a man we met at these parties.

"He will think you're easy meat," he'd said. "You know nothing about them, and you'll be vulnerable. Best to say no."

Carla had said yes, and spent a lot of time away from the flat. She didn't attend the parties and Fran and I got used to it. Toby occasionally visited and they'd disappear into her room before he left an hour or two later.

He was polite enough, but never exchanged more than a brief greeting. I tried to talk to Carla about him, but she never told us anything meaningful. All we got was how wonderful he was. Carla seemed to be smitten, but Fran and I were suspicious.

One morning, I was walking to the kitchen when Carla came out of her room, heading for the bathroom. I stopped in my tracks when I saw her face; drawn and pale, apart from the livid bruise running across her cheek up past her eye.

"Carla, are you alright?"

"Yea. Just a misunderstanding."

She went into the bathroom and bolted the door. I told Fran and we wondered what to do. When Carla returned to her room, I made a cup of coffee and knocked on her door.

"Go away," was the response.

"Carla, just take the coffee."

After a pause, the door opened but she didn't appear. I went in to find her looking at her face in the mirror.

"What happened?" I asked.

"He hit me."

"Why?"

"We were off our heads. It was an accident."

"Doesn't look like an accident."

"It was. So, forget it."

Over the coming weeks, there were a few accidents, but we couldn't get her to tell us anything. She was often bruised and became increasingly gaunt and thin.

"She's on heroin," Fran said one night when we heard her come in at three in the morning.

"How do you know?"

"I don't, but the signs are all there."

We did drugs regularly, but heroin wasn't in our repertoire. It was available at one or two of the parties we attended but as far as I knew none of the girls used it. It was one of Gordon's rules. Anyone using it didn't work for him again. I'm not sure if he was being altruistic, or if it proved bad for business.

One night, we were woken by someone banging on the door. Fran went to answer it, then called out for me. Her voice told me something was wrong. When I reached her, the front door was open, and she was trying to pull a semi-conscious Carla inside. We heard the front door of the building slam shut.

"Bastard," Fran spat out. Someone had brought Carla here, rapped the door and run off.

Between us, we hauled Carla into her room. We got her on the bed, and Fran pulled up Carla's sleeves. We looked at each other; little red marks all over her arms. Fran tried to wake her, but there was no response. She felt for a pulse.

"Call an ambulance. Quick."

While we waited, we sat on the bed next to our friend, helpless. She was alive but completely lifeless. The ambulance arrived in minutes and we told them what we knew. They did what they could to keep her stable and carried her downstairs on a stretcher. We threw some old clothes on and went with her. She was dead before we reached the hospital.

Chapter 8 - A Class Act

The police came the next day. It was clear we were suspects rather than witnesses. They asked us who supplied the heroin, where we'd got it. We told them the story; no lies, just the truth as we knew it. But we didn't know much, that was the problem. We didn't know what Carla had been doing recently or with who, and we only knew Toby by his first name.

Then one of the cops found a business card in Carla's room. Toby's card. Everything changed, and nothing changed. He turned out to be the son of a prominent businessman, well-connected and rich. The police dropped the investigation and the inquest recorded a verdict of death by misadventure. Case closed.

Carla's family came to collect her belongings and I will never forget the look on their faces; disdain, almost hatred. They blamed us for her death. I guess they never knew the truth and it's probably better that way.

Fran and I dealt with it as best we could. We were close now and the connection we had gave us strength. In the aftermath, there were several nights when one or both of us cried ourselves to sleep. It wasn't just Carla's death. It was the realisation it could have been us; that what we were doing had its dangers. We promised we'd look out for each other.

We didn't change course, though. We told Gordon about Carla, but he wasn't interested. She hadn't worked for him since being banned. We resumed the parties, but there was a melancholy to it all for me. It became a job; it paid good money, but the initial excitement had gone.

We were more careful with drugs as well, limiting ourselves to weed and a few pills. And we watched each other, not wanting to go through the pain again. I was surprised I didn't miss the coke. I'd grown blasé about the parties, about fucking any man there who wanted me. I made sure I pleased; my income depended on it. But I wasn't worried whether I enjoyed it or not. Sometimes I did, but generally, it was an act.

Not at home, though. Fran and I were good together. We got on well, particularly as I'd now developed the same cynical view of the world she had. We were enjoying life. The sex was wonderful; nothing like I'd experienced before. I was in love. We didn't advertise for a new flatmate. We were making enough to live on our own; if that meant working an extra party or two, so be it.

"Either of you been spanked?" Gordon asked one day.

We looked at him; what was he up to now?

"Not me," Fran replied.

"Nor me," I added. The memories of being slippered at school came into my head, but I ignored them.

"Pity," Gordon said.

"Why?"

"I had an idea for themed parties. One of them might be around schoolgirls. I need one or two girls to take a spanking. It'll pay well."

"Who'll do the spanking?" I asked.

Gordon smiled and leaned back in his chair.

"A guy I know who makes spanking films. He knows what he's doing."

"I might be up for it," I replied. Fran looked at me with astonishment but said nothing. "When do you need to know?"

"No hurry, it's just an idea."

As we left his office, Fran stopped me.

"Are you serious about the spanking?"

"Yea. I got corporal punishment at school. Only the slipper, but the other girls freaked out, yelling, and crying. I hardly felt it, so I guess I can take a spanking."

"You must have a high pain threshold."

"Yea. Remember our fight? My head hardly hurt."

"Hey, I was the one with the real injuries."

She grinned as she said it.

After discussing it, and seeing exactly how much it paid, we decided to try it. It made us laugh. We were told to dress as schoolgirls, but this was unlike any schoolgirl I'd ever seen. White suspenders and stockings, white knickers, a very short skirt, paired with a tight white top and heels. I managed to tie my hair in bunches, although they were rather large.

When we arrived at the venue, it was laid out like a schoolroom, right down to a few rows of old-fashioned desks. We met Dale, the man who was going to spank us. He was middle-aged, quiet, and serious, and he gave us a run-down of what he wanted us to do and what would happen.

It seemed simple enough. We pretend we'd been sent to the headmaster's office. Dale as headmaster would tell us off and give us a spanking. Gordon had already told us that if the spanking hurt too much, we could leave at that point; he'd provide enough girls to cover us.

Dale took us to a side room, and we waited for the guests and girls to arrive. After about an hour, we were told everything was ready and our show began. We realised we were going to have to act, but Dale told us not to worry; the men weren't there to enjoy our acting skills.

Which was just as well, because as soon as we went out, we had to use all our energy not to giggle. The men in the audience were each sat at a desk, with the girls perched on their laps. Dale had an academic gown on, and we bluffed our way through looking like we were guilty of something. We never did establish quite what.

Thankfully, he didn't drag it out and soon told us to bend over a table in the centre of the stage. There were a few cheers as our short skirts revealed our bums. Dale was used to this; he stood behind us and lectured us about behaviour and disgracing the school while giving us each a few slaps on the bum. At one point, I made the mistake of looking at Fran, and we both descended into a fit of giggles.

This enabled Dale to move to the next level, and he made me stand by the blackboard, while he pulled a chair centre stage and made Fran lay over his lap. He stopped the lecture and began to spank her, drawing more cheers from the audience. He wasn't messing about; Fran was letting out a cry at each stroke.

Her cries got louder when he pulled her knickers down and spanked her naked bum. I could see it was reddening all over and she was shifting on Dale's lap with each stroke. He gave her a final flurry and she let out a series of shrieks, her arm coming back to shield her stinging skin. He sent her to stand by the board and I saw she was on the verge of tears. Then he called me.

I put myself over his knees and he set straight to it. The first few slaps came as a bit of a shock, but I didn't feel much pain, just a mild stinging. I lay still and silent; Dale seemed to take this as a challenge. He pulled my knickers down earlier than he had Fran's and resumed his efforts. I looked out over the audience; the men were all watching intently. The girls were ignored. As Dale spanked me harder, I heard him breathing heavily with the effort.

It was stinging now, with some mild pain, but nothing I couldn't easily handle.

"So," Dale said, resting his hand on my bum and catching his breath. "You think you can take it, do you girl?"

"Yes, sir," came out before I knew it and I heard him stifle a laugh.

"Let's see."

And he resumed my spanking; much harder and quicker than before. This time, I could feel it. The pace was the worst, my skin unable to relax from one stroke before the next came. I found myself wriggling slightly, and he held me firmer with his free arm. But I was still silent. He came to a halt and I heard him gasping for breath.

"Right, my girl. I hope that's taught you a lesson."

"Yes, sir," I said, getting up and re-joining Fran.

The audience cheered as we took a bow and the girls finally received some attention. Dale, Fran, and I returned to the side room.

"Well," Dale said to me. "You can take it, can't you? Done this before?"

"No, this is the first time."

He gave me an appraising look.

"Interesting ..."

He bade us farewell and we were left alone.

"Want to go join the party?" I asked.

Fran looked at me and burst into tears; I put my arms around her as she clung to me. I think that meant no.

When we got home, I put her in a warm bath; she flinched as her bum met the water.

"Aren't you hurting?" she asked after she finally managed to lower herself to the bottom.

"Not much," I replied. "Stings a bit."

"He was much harder with you, but my ass hurts like hell. Show me yours."

I took my gown off and turned my back to her.

"Look in the mirror," she said.

I had to manoeuvre into position and when I did, I saw my bum was red, very red. But all I could feel was a bit of heat.

"You're not human," Fran said. "I won't be able to sit for a week."

I joined her in the bath and when we were dry, we carefully rubbed moisturiser into each other's bruised bums. What followed took Fran's mind off her pain.

"You two did well," Gordon said when we visited him a couple of days later. "Dale was impressed; especially with you, Bella."

He paid us our money; the same amount we'd have got if we'd fucked the guests.

"Up for it again?" he asked.

We'd discussed it. I was more than happy, it had been a doddle for me. Three hundred quid for half an hour's work. No drooling men panting over me, no need for alcohol or drugs to get through it. It was a bit different for Fran, she'd felt it a lot more, but she didn't say no.

Gordon set up a meeting with us and Dale, and we came up with more structure for the performance. We worked out a rough script to extend the time. Fran would take a longer spanking, with Dale making it look harder than it was, then I'd be the main attraction.

The first time we tried it, it went down a storm. We were more confident; we knew what to expect and even we were surprised by the reaction. Several of the men in the audience came and gave us tips. That had never happened after they fucked us.

Gordon arranged a couple of events every month and we also did one or two of his conventional parties. We were raking it in.

"We need to think about the future," Fran said one day after we'd collected our money from Gordon.

"I'm not ready to settle down," I replied, and she smiled.

"Not that. We're making money here. We ought to be doing something with it, not frittering it away."

I agreed; I'd been thinking the same. Things were going well, but it wouldn't last forever. God knows, I didn't want it to. We were making two grand a month and at the moment, it was accumulating in my bank account.

"Yea, but what?" I said.

"Property's best."

"Nobody's going to give us a mortgage."

"True."

"And we don't yet have enough to buy anything for cash, not even together."

We ended up asking Gordon. I was in two minds; he was astute, but I didn't fully trust him. He recommended a friend of his, which didn't help.

"Is he on the level?" I asked.

"He'd bloody well better be. He's looking after most of my money."

The friend turned out to work for a respectable investment company and he sorted out some plans which I didn't fully understand, but Fran appeared to. She was happy, so I went along with it. It was the best decision I ever made.

"I've had some feedback," Gordon said. "I want to make one or two changes."

We were sitting in his office. Our relationship with Gordon had grown into a comfortable one. We still didn't fully trust him; he probably didn't trust us. But he'd never cheated us, he always found us work and he looked after us.

"Oh, yes," Fran said. "What now?"

"You're in demand. I could run more of these things if I could find any more like you."

"Cut the crap, Gordon."

He held his hands up and grinned.

"The feedback's good, but there's one thing missing."

"What's that?"

"The men want to spank you."

"Not me," Fran replied. "No way."

I'd spent some time thinking about the audience reactions to our performance; it was clearly a common fantasy. The fact Dale made a living out of spanking films showed there was a market, and the girls who handled the men after we'd finished told us there were always a few guys who asked to spank them. They always said no, but the men were always friskier than at the regular parties.

I didn't get it, although we noticed Fran and I had some intense sex sessions when we got home.

"I'm not sure," I said. "Dale knows what he's doing and doesn't get carried away. Some arrogant little banker isn't going to be so careful when he's got me naked over his lap, is he?"

He had his head resting on his steepled fingers. For once, he was thinking rather than posing.

"And how would you do it?" I continued. "There might be a dozen of them. There's only one of me and I'm not having them lining up to slap my ass."

"But in principle, you'd think about it?"

"Yea, if I was happy with the situation and it was under control."

Chapter 9 - Screen Debut

I came up with a solution. A raffle. All the men who wanted to spank me bought a ticket and the lucky winner was selected at random. He got ten minutes. It proved popular, and not just with the guys who won.

These events tended to draw a different audience to Gordon's other parties. Those were often a random group of men in town for some common purpose, but they didn't always know each other. The themed events attracted groups; a few stag parties, friends celebrating someone's birthday.

So, when a guy got to spank me, his mates were all cheering him on. Generally, the atmosphere was lighter. Even the other girls told us they enjoyed them more. By the time the sex started, the guys tended to be in party mood and more amenable.

It made me extra money; good extra money for doing something I was indifferent to. Some of the winners were overwhelmed; they wanted to do it but had no idea what they were doing and ended up giving my bum a few playful slaps. A few had clearly done it before. Only once did our security guy have to step in when one man seemed to think he had free rein and started by slapping my face.

Gordon was happy; I'd agreed to give him twenty per cent of the raffle pot, and it made the parties even more popular.

He upped the prices, and nobody complained. He'd branched out and stopped the Selwood Terrace parties.

"They don't make any money," he complained. We doubted that was true, but they did take a lot of time and weren't worth the effort. He still organised girls for parties whenever they were needed, they were the core business. Now he had the themed parties. The schoolgirl ones we were involved in, another with maids serving the guests, and anything else reasonable if a client requested it.

I wondered how he fitted everything in. We'd never met any staff, he seemed to work alone. But he was efficient and looked after his girls. I'd only ever seen a handful of occasions where things got out of hand, but the security guy had always waded in, sorted it out and looked after the girl involved.

Before a performance one evening, Dale took us to one side.

"How would you two like to make some extra money?"

"How?"

"You know I make spanking films?"

"Yea, Gordon told us."

"Make a film with me. We could do what we do here."

We said we'd think about it. It seemed easy enough, but there were differences. These parties were closed, a dozen guys at most. They wouldn't recognise us if we passed them in the street tomorrow. But on film? It would be seen anywhere and be around forever.

Life was good; Fran and I were happy, and we had money with plenty of time to enjoy it. We did things and visited places we couldn't have dreamed of if we'd worked in ordinary jobs. But we knew the work was taking its toll. We'd grown cynical, particularly about men. We knew a lot of those who spanked me or fucked us were married or involved.

We knew we took risks. AIDs was everywhere; in the news, in adverts. Everyone was aware of it, but few understood it. It was still being called the gay plague by the more frenzied sections of the press. We knew different. It didn't matter who you fucked or how, you were vulnerable if you weren't careful. Sometimes, that didn't save you.

Checking a guy was fully covered was second nature to us, but it wasn't foolproof. We'd heard of girls still getting HIV. It was scary but ultimately didn't stop us. We just hoped we'd be lucky.

We were on the edges of society. We didn't mix outside our circle; trying to explain what we did, or lying about it, was hard work. And girls doing what we did were always vulnerable to violence. We knew if we were hurt, it was useless reporting it; the police would be more likely to prosecute us.

We talked a lot about what we'd do afterwards. Afterwards was always a vague concept and we were careful to avoid defining it. But every girl I knew had a plan, some more realistic than others; few of us were destined to achieve them.

Fran and I changed our plans every other week, but we were building some resources for the future and it gave us hope. We didn't talk about our relationship much. We were in love, but we never analysed it too deeply.

We arrived at the address Dale had given us, a warehouse on the outskirts of Croydon. He'd lent us a couple of his films to see what they were like; this had caused an outbreak of hilarity. They were like the performance we put on, but the acting was so awful, we couldn't work out how anyone took them seriously.

He offered us eight hundred pounds each to do something we were doing two or three times a month for less than half that. It was too good to refuse.

"Hi, girls, come through."

He led us through an empty space to a door off a corridor, into a schoolroom. Rather an inaccurate one, but recognisable, nonetheless.

"This is Terry. He's the cameraman."

"Hi," Terry said, not taking his eyes off the camera he was fiddling with.

"You can change in the toilet," Dale said. "It's not very luxurious, I'm afraid."

He was right; it was clean, but that was about it. We got changed and went back to the schoolroom. Dale explained the process and it turned out to be the least erotic thing I'd ever done. We recreated our usual performance almost word for word, but we had to stop all the time to change position or to allow Terry to shoot from a different angle.

It took most of the day, but at the end, Dale gave us our money and promised to give us a copy when they'd edited it.

"Do you want your names on it, or shall I make up something?" he asked.

We hadn't thought about it, but eventually decided he could use our first names. What did it matter?

We watched the finished video a couple of weeks later; in silence to begin with. It was odd seeing yourself on screen as other people saw you. We commented on each other's performance; poking fun and picking up the little mistakes we hadn't bothered to correct.

By the end, we were silent again. Watching myself naked and exposed had got me hot. For the first time, I saw the appeal. I couldn't explain it, but it turned me on. When I looked at Fran, she was looking at me, smiling.

"What?" I said.

"Come here."

The video had had the same effect on her. We ripped each other's clothes off and had some of the roughest sex we'd ever had.

The phone rang early one morning; it was Gordon.

"Don't come to the office," he told us. "Meet me at eleven in the coffee bar on the corner of Highland Road."

We were puzzled; Gordon didn't usually do cloak and dagger stuff. We got dressed, had breakfast, and set off to find out what was going on.

"They released me on bail," Gordon said, after telling his tale. He was unshaven and not his usual dapper self. He'd been arrested the previous afternoon for supplying Class A drugs. It was a serious charge.

"What happens now?" Fran asked.

"I'm not sure what they've got on me, but if any of the girls have talked, I'm in the shit."

"Do you still supply, Gordon?" I asked.

"Not anymore. With the Selwood Terrace gig gone, there's no need. I don't supply the stuff at the parties."

"Are you on anything?"

He gave a hollow laugh and looked a little guilty for the first time since I'd known him.

"Not on your nelly. I'm not that stupid."

He could be a bastard, but I liked him.

"So, everything grinds to a halt?" Fran asked. "We're all unemployed."

"Afraid so."

"Not necessarily," I said. He narrowed his eyes and gave me a calculating look.

"What do you mean?" Fran said.

"Why have you asked us here, Gordon?" I asked.

"To tell you the news."

"Why us? Why not the other girls?"

"I've got a soft spot for you."

"Bollocks. You've never had a soft spot for anyone but yourself."

A sly grin appeared on his face and he leaned forward.

"All right," he said. "You two are smart; I've seen that. You look after yourselves, you don't snort or drink the profits and you've got ideas. The other girls come and go, but you've stuck to it and pulled your weight."

"And?"

"Want to help me out?"

"How?

He was honest; he had a previous conviction for pimping. If he were found guilty on the drugs charge, he could be sent down for years. His business would collapse, and he wanted to avoid that. That's where we came in.

"Keep it going," he said. "Nothing flash, nothing new. Just keep me in business."

"Don't you have anyone to do it for you?"

"Nah. I've had partners in the past and we've always fallen out over something."

"But how do you survive in this business on your own?" Fran asked. "There's a lot of competition."

He sighed and sat back in his chair.

"Ever heard of Sonny Luckett?" he asked.

Had we heard of him? He was a local businessman, and by reputation, not entirely legitimate. He was known and respected throughout the area, but nobody crossed him. Quite why, I didn't know, but I could guess.

"Yea, I've heard of him."

"He's my cousin."

"So, he looks after you," Fran said.

"In a way. Not actively, but everyone knows he wouldn't take kindly if anything happened to me."

"Do you pay him?" I asked.

He looked offended for a moment, then smiled.

"I do him the odd favour. If he needs girls for a party, I supply them and pick up the bill."

"Nothing else?"

"Nah. That's about it."

"Is that the whole truth? I'm not getting involved with anything heavy."

"It's the truth, Bella. Swear it. Just don't do anything to offend him. I'm going to need all the friends I've got."

I looked at Fran and she nodded.

"What's in it for us?" I asked.

"Half the profits while you're looking after things."

"Okay, Gordon. I'm sure we're going to regret this, but what do you want us to do?"

He spent the next half an hour going through how he ran things. It was all personal contacts, word of mouth and cash.

There was a lot to take in, but he gave us his notebook. Details of all the girls, past and present. Party hosts, venue owners. It was packed with contacts.

"I'm going to keep a low profile for a bit," he said. "I've got a place out in the sticks; this is the number. If you need me, call. And call me every day to keep me up to date. Don't give that number to anyone."

"Right," I said. "The first thing we need to do is call all the girls."

"Why?" he said.

"They'll need to know, Gordon, and we need to know if they'll work for us."

"Yea, I suppose so."

He gave us the keys to the office.

"Don't lose them, and don't make copies," he said.

"Gordon ..."

"Yea."

"Advice we can always use, but don't treat us like idiots. If you're trusting us with this, cut us some slack."

"Sorry, I'm feeling a bit rough."

"Go to the sticks, have a shower ... and a shave. Then relax. We'll handle it."

As we separated in the street, I tried to convince myself we could.

Chapter 10 - Girls in Charge

"Good morning."

The speaker was standing at the door, looking around the office. We hadn't had any visitors in our first two days except some of the other girls. Gordon didn't welcome uninvited guests and the office was well off the beaten track. The man took a couple of steps into the room and another guy slipped in behind him, closing the door.

"Good morning," I replied, glancing at Fran. "Can I help you?"

"Not really," he said and ambled across the room, before sitting in the chair on the other side of the desk. He was immaculately dressed and supremely sure of himself. The silence was deafening as he took a long look at me, before appraising Fran in the same way.

"So, you're Annabelle," he said. "And you must be Francesca."

I had a feeling who I was dealing with and was determined not to yield.

"We may be," I replied. "And you are ...?"

He crossed his legs and brushed a non-existent speck from his trousers.

"I'm Sonny."

My guess was right.

"Ah, I thought we might be honoured with a visit."

He gave me a brief smile.

"Gordon was right," he said.

"About what?"

"He said you could look after yourself."

"I've had to."

"Good. Keeps you on your toes."

I was fed up with this game.

"What can we do for you, Sonny?"

"I thought I'd come and introduce myself. Gordon's family, and I always look after family. So, I'll make it brief. Gordon thinks you two can handle this; I'm not so sure. I wouldn't let two girls run anything. But he's always trusted his instincts and I like that, so we'll see. If you need any help, call me. I'll do what I can. But don't make a mess of it."

"Is that a threat?"

"No, Annabelle," he replied, a wounded smile coming to his face. "It's some free ... advice."

"Thank you, Sonny. We'll bear it in mind, but we don't intend to make a mess of it. I do have one or two questions, though."

"Fire away."

We had a brief discussion. Since taking over, we'd found out a lot more about Gordon's business. There wasn't much in the office; a couple of phone lines, some account books and a safe.

The girls were nearly all fine with us taking over for a while; as long as they got work and were paid, they didn't care who was in charge. A couple cried off, and two more wouldn't speak to us; we guessed they were the ones who shopped Gordon.

He found the girls mainly by word of mouth. There were lots of women doing what we did across London and Gordon picked the best he could find. His reputation attracted them. He was known to be fair and straightforward and provided regular work. He also looked after them and we found out Sonny had a hand in that.

The security guys at the parties were his men; Gordon paid them, but Sonny recommended them. We assumed if Sonny recommended someone or something, you took the advice. He was happy to continue the arrangement.

"I run a security company," he said, "amongst other things. Bouncers, close protection, guards; you name it, we do it. We can always find people for you."

"I'd be happy to keep the existing team; the girls all know them and that makes them feel safer."

"No problem; Dave's your contact. Any problems, speak to him. He'll be here shortly."

Sure enough, as Sonny left with his associate, Dave came through the door.

"Morning, you two," he said.

"Morning, Dave. Something tells me we need to talk."

It turned out Dave was more than a heavy; he was Gordon's gopher. He wasn't the smartest card in the pack but give him clear instructions and he followed them to the letter. He collected the money from whoever was hiring the girls and brought it safely to the office. He spoke to the other security guys after every party and reported back to Gordon. How it had gone, which girls hadn't pulled their weight, which ones had been popular, who had gone overboard with the alcohol or drugs.

"Isn't it frustrating, Dave?" Fran asked. "Sitting in the corner watching other people fuck?"

He grinned.

"Nah. Now if it was a bunch of handsome young men ..."

She'd been right, he was perfect for the job. We came to rely heavily on his advice and his knowledge of the whole process. Gordon paid him well, and so did we.

Fran and I stopped working the parties ourselves and concentrated on organising things and dealing with the day to day admin. It proved easier than we'd anticipated, but we had one or two setbacks. One of the regular clients didn't take kindly to dealing with us and decided to find his own girls.

"He'll be back," Dave assured us. He was right. Ten days later, the guy called us. He'd hosted two parties in the meantime and sourced the girls himself. It had been a disaster; they simply weren't as good. We agreed to work with him again but raised the price. He fumed but paid up.

"He always was a tosser," Gordon said when we told him. We'd come some way out of London to meet him in a pub. We spoke every day, but the cash in the safe was mounting up and he'd told us to bring the excess to him. "He's a good organiser; he's been one of my – our – best customers. But he always thinks he can get a better deal."

"Not this time, he couldn't."

Gordon chuckled.

"It was a bit risky upping the price," he said.

"He couldn't say no, he'd have been scuppered."

"Yea, but be careful."

"Any news?" Fran asked.

He slumped in his chair.

"I've been charged with possession; they can't prove I sold it to anyone, 'cos I didn't. They know I was giving it to you lot, but they're not pursuing it."

"Why not?"

"Because they don't trust the evidence of the two bitches who've shopped me. Probably get thrown out of court."

"Tracy and Wendy?"

"Yea, how did you know?"

"They were the only two girls who wouldn't talk to us."

"Ah."

"So," Fran said. "They'd rather get you for something than risk the case collapsing."

"Yes."

"What are you going to do?"

"Already done it. Gonna plead guilty."

"Will that help?"

"Solicitor thinks it'll be dealt with by the magistrate's court. They can only put you away for twelve months."

"Bad enough."

"Better than three or four years."

We fell into a melancholy silence. After we passed the cash over in the car park, Fran and I went home. For the first time, I thought about prison, realising what we were doing could get us sent down as well. It wasn't a pleasant thought.

After he pleaded guilty, the case came quickly. He'd been right, no evidence was submitted, no witnesses called. His previous conviction was noted, and the magistrates fined him a thousand pounds and sent him to prison for ten months. With good behaviour, he'd be out in seven. We had work to do.

We had everything down to a fine art now and decided to restart the themed parties. They proved as popular as before and we finally found a couple of other girls to perform as well. It was Dale who introduced them; they had done some films for him. Cassie and Della were experienced spankees, but they were initially put off by what else went on at the parties. They weren't interested in selling themselves.

That was fair enough; we knew it wasn't for everyone. But Dale invited them to attend one of the events Fran and I did. They watched our performance, and what was going on in the audience. When we all left, they were a bit unsure but decided to give it a try.

This time, it was our turn to watch and they acquitted themselves well. Both could act and take a hard spanking; the audience loved it. When we talked to them afterwards, they were happy to repeat the performance and they became a part of the team. Cassie was to become a good friend in the coming years.

Although he told us not to bother, we visited Gordon in prison. We suspected he had no other visitors. It was a depressing place; it was meant to be. But he seemed to be coping well. I wondered if it were known he had connections, which would protect him from being hassled.

He seemed happy with our success, although he always had advice for us, most of it unnecessary, but we humoured him.

"What do we do with the excess cash, Gordon?" I asked. The money piling up in the safe was making me uneasy. He studied us for some time, before making a decision.

"There's a set of keys in the safe with a 'T' painted on them. Tell Dave to take you to the Tadworth house. He'll know what to do."

We bundled up the cash and Dave drove us out to the suburbs, where he turned into a rough lane between two shops. At the end of the track, we came to a detached house, standing alone between the trees. I opened the front door and got something of a shock. The interior was immaculate; trendy décor and plush furniture, with some stunning art on the walls. Much of it pornographic.

"Is this where Gordon lives?" Fran asked Dave. He shrugged, sheepishly, but no answer came. He led us to the under stairs cupboard and opened the door. Lifting a hidden latch, he swung the floor open, revealing a set of steps. We followed him and he turned a light on at the bottom, illuminating a small cellar. It was empty, apart from two safes, standing against the wall.

I assumed the keys I had contained those for the safes.

"Any idea, Dave?"

"No, I've never been down here before."

I realised Dave must be visiting Gordon in prison. We'd have to be careful; he was a godsend to us, but clearly still reporting to Gordon.

I tried the keys until I found one that fitted the first safe. Pulling the door open I was confronted with bundles of cash; I couldn't even guess how much. I put what we'd brought on top and locked the safe again.

"Is someone looking after this place while Gordon's away?" I asked. He'd been inside for over two months, yet this house had been cleaned since then.

"Yes," was the only response we got from Dave. On the way back, I wondered why Gordon hadn't just got Dave to bring the money out and hide it. Why involve Fran and me?

"Security," Gordon replied when I asked him at our next visit.

"Security?"

"When other people are running around with my money, I prefer to have more than one person involved. Then nobody's going to get any ideas, are they?"

"Don't you trust anyone?" I asked.

"Do you?"

One evening, Fran and I talked about our plans. We still didn't discuss our personal relationship; I think we were too scared. We were enjoying being together and didn't want to think too hard. But financially we were doing well. When we'd taken over his business, we saw how much Gordon was making. He paid the girls around three hundred pounds for working at a party.

But he charged five hundred, so if he provided six girls, which was the average, he made twelve hundred. Not bad for one evening. And he was providing girls for at least two parties a week, as well as the themed ones. We were running all this now and the profit averaged three thousand a week. Half of that was ours, plus what we earned; it seemed unreal.

"What are we going to do with it all?" Fran asked.

"We could put more in the investment plans."

"Yea. But come on, Bella. We don't want to do this forever. I want to get out at some point, I'm getting nervous."

I knew what she meant. The work was easy enough. We had a good group of loyal girls, a few party hosts who wanted our services and the themed parties were a huge success. But the whole thing was precarious, Gordon's arrest had proved that. Everything we did was either illegal or on the verge of illegality. It was wearing; we were always unsure what tomorrow might bring.

Chapter 11 - Locked Up

Gordon was released after serving just over seven months. We went with Dave to pick him up from prison. He came out somewhat thinner than he went in, but other than that, he seemed his usual self.

"What's this?" he asked when he got into the car. "A bloody welcoming committee?"

"We wanted to make sure you're alright," I replied. "Don't be so ungrateful."

He gave me a shrewd look.

"I'm not, Bella. You've done well, both of you. I'm almost sorry to take it all over again."

So were we. While he'd been inside, Fran and I hadn't had to work any of the parties. We'd done the schoolgirl performances, but we hadn't sold ourselves for nearly nine months. We hadn't been too upset about that. We knew he'd take over again, and we'd have to go back to our old work if we wanted to keep the money rolling in. But once again, fate intervened.

Gordon took a break for a few days. We dropped him off at his house in Tadworth and went back to the office. We'd made sure the books were all up to date and had left them with him, to go through. It proved a lucky break because the next morning, the office door was kicked open and four policemen burst in.

Fran and I were cautioned and had to watch while they searched the premises. We looked at each other a couple of times. Fran had a resigned look on her face; I guess my expression matched hers. We were in the shit.

They took us to the local station, where we were arrested for a variety of offences, but all revolved around prostitution and running a brothel. We'd discussed how we would answer such charges because it was always a possibility and we'd worked out our answers. We wouldn't deny involvement, but we would be economical with the truth.

They released us on bail the following morning. Shortly after we got home, Gordon rang.

"I heard," he said. "What happened?"

We told him what we'd been asked and how we replied.

"Good," he said. "I'm sending you my solicitor."

When he arrived later in the afternoon, we had a long discussion about the charges and how to respond. He knew everything about Gordon's business and didn't mess around. There was no way we were getting out of this unscathed; it was all about mitigating the damage.

Over the next few weeks, we discovered it was Tracy and Wendy who'd landed us in it again. What they had against us, or Gordon, we never discovered. They'd never worked for us, and the other girls went to ground, or wouldn't say anything, and the books weren't in the office when it was raided.

In the end, we could only be charged with living off immoral earnings and procuring women to engage in prostitution. We pleaded guilty to the first but denied the second. When the case came to court, Tracy and Wendy's unreliability worked to our advantage again.

We admitted we were paid to find girls to act as hostesses at parties and took a cut of the fees.

"Hostesses?" the magistrate asked.

"Yes, sir," I replied.

"For the purposes of providing sex to the guests," he said.

"What the girls did was up to them, sir."

He gave me a wry smile; we both knew I wasn't telling the whole truth, but he seemed satisfied not to pursue it.

"But you knew the girls would have sex with the men?" he asked.

"I assumed they didn't sit around discussing interest rates, sir."

I saw our solicitor look away to avoid his smile being too obvious. Fran and I told broadly the same story, though not too close as to look coached. Tracy was called as a witness. This was the first time I'd seen her since she shopped Gordon, and I instantly remembered her.

She'd been at one or two of the earliest parties I'd attended. I recalled her causing a fuss about something and swearing at one of the guests. She told the court how she worked at the parties, having sex in return for the money she would be paid.

"So, you were paid by my clients?" our solicitor asked.

"Nah," she replied. "I wouldn't work for them."

The magistrate looked puzzled.

"So," he asked. "The defendants have never paid you to have sex with the men at these events?"

"No."

Her story fell apart rapidly after that. The magistrate refused to listen to anything else from her and upbraided the police solicitor for wasting time. Wendy was called and the same thing happened. She tried to bring Gordon into the story.

"Young lady," the magistrate said. "The man you mention is not on trial in this court. Did the defendants pay you to have sex with men?"

"No."

He dismissed her as well and asked if the prosecutor wanted to pursue both charges. After some discussion, the procuring charge was dropped.

"I'm not sure the court has heard the whole story behind this case," the magistrate concluded. "But the defendants have pleaded guilty to the charge of living off immoral earnings. The sums of money found in their office would indicate those earnings were substantial.

"But I can only sentence you on the evidence presented to me today, which," he said, looking sourly at the prosecutor, "has been somewhat woeful. I sentence you both to six weeks in prison and a fine of two thousand pounds."

Fran and I were sent to different prisons. I planned to keep my head down, it was only a few weeks. It reminded me of boarding school, very regimented with an undercurrent of bullying and trading favours. I wouldn't be in long enough to establish a place in the pecking order.

At the end of the first week, I was having a shower when two women came in. I'd seen one of them before and noticed she was deferred to by the other inmates.

"Well, at least the colour's natural," she said as she passed me. My pubic hair was almost as red as that on my head.

They went to the other end of the communal shower and stripped off. The leader was in her early thirties; well-built and muscular, without an ounce of spare flesh. Attractive in a severe way. The other woman was younger and prettier, with a tempting figure. She proceeded to wash her boss, soaping her, and rubbing her down.

I carried on with my shower and saw she was watching me as she was being washed. Her look told me why. She was looking at my body, letting her eyes rest on my breasts and between my legs. After the last few years, modesty was something I wasn't familiar with. I decided to play her game.

Without looking at her, I ran my hands over my body, letting the water cascade over me. I missed Fran, and thoughts of her soon got to work. I leaned back against the wall and let one hand run between my legs, gently rubbing and spreading my sex. When I looked at my companion, she had responded.

She too was leaning against the wall, with her helper kneeling in front of her, her face buried in muscle woman's groin. She seemed to know what she was doing, as my challenger was enjoying it. We watched each other as we came towards release, coming at virtually the same time. My orgasm was brief and quiet. Hers was louder, as she pulled the girl's face into her.

When the moment passed, we both washed again and stepped out to dry off. As she rubbed herself down, she walked towards me. I wondered if I'd got myself into something I couldn't control; she was heavier than me and looked far stronger.

"Well," she said in a sarcastic drawl. "Who have we here?"

"Bella," I answered as flatly as I could.

"Let me see ... she's got red hair, she's called Bella and she thinks she can look after herself. He said I'd recognise you."

"He?"

"A friend of mine. You'll be okay in here." She turned to her companion. "Come on Gina, we haven't got all day."

The other girl quickly dried herself as we got dressed. I didn't know whether to pursue the discussion; the decision was made for me as she got ready to leave. She stopped as she drew level with me.

"I'm Kara, by the way," she said. "Don't believe everything you hear about me."

She walked out of the shower room, Gina racing to keep up. I dressed and returned to my cell. It had been a strange meeting. I began to understand her last piece of advice when I asked around about her. Kara was treated with respect by just about everyone, though nobody could tell me exactly why. She was someone important; she was a vicious murderer; she could beat the shit out of anyone. I got a variety of answers; all turned out to be wrong.

Gina turned up in my cell one day.

"Kara wants you to sign up for a gym session," she said, throwing a small bundle of cloth on the bed and leaving. I'd never been to a gym in my life; the obsession had never gripped me. But I had no choice; I'd guessed Kara's connection on the outside, and I wanted to be sure.

The bundle turned out to be something to wear in the gym; a pair of thigh-length lycra shorts and a crop-top. I smiled as I imagined Kara's reasons for giving them to me, but also wondered how she got them. I found the hobbies board and signed up for the next class.

The gym wasn't exactly purpose-built, it looked like an old storeroom. It had been given a coat of paint and the floor was covered with thin mats. There were three exercise bikes, two rowing machines, some weights, and wall-bars. When I walked in, Kara was on one of the bikes. She stopped and took a long look at my body, smiling as she did so.

"You took my advice," she said.

"I'm always open to advice," I replied, mounting the bike beside her. She laughed as I pushed the pedals, and nothing happened; they didn't move.

"I can see you're not a regular," she said, leaning over and turning a knob several times, allowing the pedals to rotate.

"Never been in one in my life."

"It shows."

There were one or two other people in the room, and I noticed they were surreptitiously glancing at us. I guessed they were trying to find out who this new girl was. Gina was squatting on the floor a few feet away; she was clearly Kara's gopher.

"Who's your friend, then?" I asked.

"Gina?"

"No. You know who I mean."

"Sonny."

"Thought so."

"He looks after his friends."

"Not sure I'm a friend, I've only met him once."

"Perhaps. But I'm told you helped someone in his family. He remembers things like that."

She was talking as she worked the bike steadily. The sweat was running down her face and I wasn't sure why. The pedals were so easy to push around, it was almost too easy. She saw my puzzlement and reached over, turning the knob again, smiling when I lost momentum as the resistance increased.

"Heard anything about Fran?" I asked. I'd been thinking about her a lot.

"Not much. Sonny tried, but he hasn't got anyone in there at the moment."

It was disappointing, but she'd be all right. She was tough and self-confident; she could look after herself.

"She's an interesting one, is Kara," Gordon said. "You two should get on well."

He came to visit me after the second week; I was surprised and hadn't expected it.

"What's she in for?" I said. "There are so many rumours."

"Ask her."

"Not exactly the done thing, is it?"

"She won't mind."

"I'll think about it. Are you in touch with Sonny?"

"Yea, all the time."

"Thank him for me, will you?"

"Sure."

"Have you seen Fran?" I asked. His face darkened momentarily.

"Yea, I saw her yesterday."

"Is she okay?"

He let out a sigh.

"Not doing as well as you."

"Why?"

"She was very down. Cried a couple of times while I was there."

I was shocked, I couldn't remember her crying. I felt sure he wasn't telling me everything, but I didn't push. I didn't want the extra weight on me; there was nothing I could do.

"How's business?" I asked.

He gave a hollow laugh.

"What business?"

"What's wrong?"

"I've shut up shop."

"No."

"Yea. We ... I've been lucky. But when they got me, I should have thought it through. They knew what was going on, they just needed a way to shut me down. They got me on the drugs charge, then when I come out, they get you two on the pimping charge. It's too hot to carry on."

"The girls?"

"They know the score; they'll find work with someone else."

"What are you going to do?"

"I'm retiring."

"Seriously? I can't imagine you retiring."

"Come on, I'm not getting any younger. You saw what I was making; you saw the safes. I've made decent money for years and I haven't wasted it. It's all been salted away. I've got enough to live comfortably."

He saw my crestfallen look.

"You wanted to carry on when you come out?" he asked.

"I don't know, Gordon. I'm a lot younger than you."

"But you did stash some away, right?"

"Yes, thankfully. But it's not enough for me to live comfortably forever. I'll need to find something to do."

Chapter 12 - The Split

"What are the rumours?" Kara asked.

"Everything from jaywalking to mass murder."

She gave a low chuckle. We were on the bikes again. I'd got the hang of them now and a good session sweating in the gym made me feel better. Life inside was boring; thinking of all the things you could be doing elsewhere. Taking it out in physical exercise was a release.

"It's so easy to spread gossip amongst small minds," she said.

"You started all those stories?"

"Yup."

"Why?"

"Seen anyone hassling me?"

"No, they wouldn't dare."

"Exactly."

"But they wouldn't because of Sonny, surely?"

"Most don't know of the connection."

"Oh ..."

"I can look after myself, but I try to avoid aggro. If you can make people wary of you, they find easier targets."

"I thought people didn't hassle me because of the Sonny connection."

"People don't hassle you because I let it be known you were under my protection. That's enough."

"Come on, then. What are you in for?"

"Same as you," she replied. I stopped cycling and looked at her. "Well, more or less."

"More or less?"

"Immoral earnings, running a brothel, not declaring income. That sort of thing."

"How long did you get?"

"Twelve months."

"How long left?"

"About three if I behave myself."

"What are you going to do when you get out?"

"Who knows? I can't start up again unless I want to be back in here. What about you?"

"God knows."

The flat was musty; nobody had visited in the month I'd been inside. I opened all the windows, made myself a cup of tea and enjoyed the freedom to lounge about in private. I was looking forward to sleeping in my own bed, but the relief at being released was tempered by thoughts of tomorrow.

Fran was being released and I was going to pick her up. But something had changed. Gordon had visited her every week, but he'd been cagey about his visits. All he said seemed to indicate she'd had some sort of breakdown. I'd written to her, but after the first reply, I hadn't received anything else. It wasn't promising.

As I parked the car, I didn't know what to expect. She'd been such a big part of my life for nearly three years. Perhaps naively, I thought we would go back to how we were. As soon as I saw her, I knew that wasn't going to happen.

She came through the door carrying her bags and looked around. I got out of the car and waved. There was no response; she turned and walked slowly towards me. I went to hug her, but she turned away, put her things on the back seat and got in.

"Fran?" I said. I didn't know what else to say.

"Take me home."

The journey passed in silence and when we reached the flat, she took her bags into one of the spare rooms. I tried to talk to her but got one-word answers. It was as if she was sleepwalking; there was no emotion, no life. She went into the bedroom and I didn't see her for hours.

When she came out, I offered to cook something.

"Whatever."

"Fran, what's wrong? Talk to me."

"What about?"

"You're not yourself. What happened?"

"I never want to go through that again."

"We won't. We'll find something else to do."

She turned to me, her eyes frighteningly red.

"What?" she snapped. "What else is there? We don't know anything else, we've got no other skills. We sell ourselves to the highest bidder. They spank us, fuck us, who cares? What sort of life is that?"

I was shocked by the outburst.

"We can look- "

"No," she said. "I'm fed up with it. You've gone along with everything as if it's a game. It's not a game. It's my life and I don't want this anymore. I'm out."

I sat there, stunned. Unsure of what to say.

"Fran, we did everything together. We were good together."

"Not anymore."

My world was collapsing again. The thing that had kept me together inside was the thought of Fran and me rebuilding our lives. I'd spent so many nights dreaming about our first night back together; how much I wanted her. To feel her body next to mine, entwined in passion.

I tried to talk to her, tried to understand what had changed. Had she been bullied or attacked inside? She wouldn't answer. Had she been ill? She wouldn't answer. But one thing was clear; she blamed me for the situation. Her bitterness was directed at me. By the end of the evening, I felt helpless. I didn't understand; didn't know why I was the focus of her anger.

I hoped a good night's sleep would help; it didn't. I hoped a few days at home would help; it didn't. She went out most days on her own, returning in the evening and more or less ignoring me. Whenever I tried to talk to her, she walked away. It was beginning to upset me.

It was Fran who resolved the situation. One evening, she came home and stood in the doorway to the lounge.

"I've found somewhere to live," she said flatly. "I'm moving out tomorrow."

I wasn't surprised, but it didn't hurt any less. And it hurt more because I didn't understand why it was happening. Could I have done any more? I don't know. I've thought about it in the years since, and still don't understand it.

The next day, she gathered all her personal belongings together and piled them in the car.

"What furniture do you want?" I asked.

"Nothing. I've got all I need."

My head was spinning. We'd bought a lot of stuff for the flat, yet she was only taking her clothes and a few personal effects?

"Fran, be sensible. All this is as much yours as mine."

"It's all yours now. I'm keeping the car."

With that, she turned to leave.

"Is that it?" I asked. "You're just going?"

She turned back, a vacant look on her face. She wasn't the Fran I fell in love with.

"Yea."

"I hope you find something," I said. It was a banal thing to say, but I couldn't think of anything else in the moment.

"You too."

She walked out of the flat; I never saw her again.

I shut myself in for a week, trying to come to terms with what happened. I went through grief, anger, disbelief, and pain in that time. But in the end, I had to get out. The flat itself held too many memories. I went to visit Kara; she smiled when she came into the visiting room.

"I wondered who it was," she said, sitting the other side of the table. "I don't get visitors; I thought the screw was winding me up. Why the hell have you come to see me? Nothing better to do?"

In between tears, I told her what had happened with Fran.

"Being inside affects people in different ways," she said. "For some, it's an enforced holiday, but for others? They can't handle it."

"But Fran was always strong. She was the one who gave me my confidence back."

"Looks like she lost hers."

It was a harsh reply, but a fair appraisal.

"What are you going to do now?" she asked.

"I've no idea. No job, no friends, no idea."

She smiled and leaned forward.

"Short of money?"

"No." Thankfully, that wasn't a problem.

"Then chill. Take some time off. When was the last time you took a couple of weeks for you?"

"Can't remember."

"Then do it. And think about moving. Find somewhere new, settle in. Something will turn up."

The advice made sense; I wasn't happy in the flat anymore.

"You don't need to come," she said as visiting time came to an end.

"I know, but I'd like to. If it's okay."

"Yea," she replied, smiling. "It's okay."

I took her advice and found a new flat; smaller, but quieter. I spent the next three weeks moving in and making it a home. My first home on my own.

"Better?" Kara asked when I told her.

"Yea. It's good. Thank you."

"What for?"

"The advice."

"You're smart; you'd have thought of it. I just nudged."

I got a letter from my late father's solicitor. My twenty-fifth birthday was approaching, and they wanted to make arrangements to pay me the proceeds of my trust fund. Once again, I'd forgotten it. They sent me a cheque on the day, and I was gobsmacked; just under thirty thousand pounds. I sat in a chair, holding the letter with the cheque stapled to it, looking at it every few minutes, unable to take it in. My father may have let me down in every other way, but he came up trumps financially.

With the money I had invested, and now this, I was building a nice foundation for the future. But I didn't yet know what that future was and didn't want to fritter it away. I needed to find something to do.

"What can you do?" Kara asked when I next visited her. I didn't tell her about the inheritance.

"Not much. I went to uni but got chucked out."

"Because of the parties?"

"Yea."

"Bummer."

"Yup."

"So, you've only done sex work."

"Yes, and a few films."

"Films?"

"Spanking films."

Her face suddenly changed; a keen interest etched across it.

"What?"

I told her about the themed parties, Dale, and his films. She listened intently.

"I think I've met Dale," she said. "Middle-aged, slightly tubby, balding?"

"Yea, sounds like Dale."

"Enjoy doing them?"

I shrugged.

"It's okay. But it's boring and they're not very good."

"Can you take more than a spanking?"

"Don't know; never tried. Why?"

"Are you happy going into a porn shop?"

"I don't think it'll harm my reputation now."

"Look for any films in a series called 'Punished Pretties'."

"Punished Pretties?" I said, smiling.

"Yea, terrible title, I know. But take a look."

I wandered down to Soho the next day and found one of the dwindling number of sex shops. They were gradually disappearing; not from punitive action, but because Soho was trendy now. Other businesses could better afford the ever-rising rents. Scanning the shelves, I was amazed to see one of my films. But it stood out as poor quality; a cheap cover with a blurred picture.

I finally found a couple of Punished Pretties. They were more eye-catching, with clear pictures and better text. I chose one and took it home. It was in a different league. A much better set, better lighting and editing; even some music. But it was also a different league in content. The two girls were attractive and the guy punishing them was good too, and the action was far harder than my tame films.

There were three chapters to the film. All went way beyond a spanking; belts and canes figured prominently. The girls were left with some heavy marks and bruising, and although there was no sex, there was plenty of fingering and explicit shots.

As I watched, I found myself getting turned on. Each stroke caused a reaction in my own body, my muscles tensing as it landed. It was as if I wanted the girl to feel the pain; enjoyed her suffering. I'd stripped off and given myself an orgasm well before the end.

"What did you think?" Kara asked.

"They're a step up in quality."

"Not what I meant."

"They're quite good."

"Could you do it?"

I'd thought about that since watching it and re-watching it. Just to make sure. Three times.

"Possibly," I replied. "I don't know."

"I know the guy who makes them."

"Somehow I thought you might."

She gave me a knowing grin.

"I'm out in three weeks. I can introduce you."

"Can't do any harm to meet him."

"He'll like you; you're stunning."

I was surprised by the obvious compliment and it showed, making her laugh.

"Come on, Bella. Remember the showers? It wasn't just Gina getting me off."

"I thought you were going to give me a beating."

"I was testing you, well, teasing you."

"Did I pass?"

"Pass? I didn't expect you to frig yourself off. You won that little contest."

Chapter 13 - Seeking Employment

Kara had given me the address, but like Gordon's before, I couldn't find it. It seemed easy enough, the numbers ran consecutively down the street, but number fifty-seven was missing. Then I spotted an alleyway a few houses further on; worth a try.

As the lane reached the back of the houses, there was a doorway to one side with an intercom. No number, no name; just the intercom panel. I pressed the button.

"Hello?" a rather indistinct voice said.

"Kara?"

The door buzzed and I pushed it open. I found myself at the bottom of a flight of stairs, Kara was standing at the top.

"Come on up," she said.

When I reached her, she gave me a hug and a peck on the cheek.

"You found it."

"Eventually. Was that a test, as well?"

"Not really, I just forgot."

"You're well-hidden here."

"Yea, that's the idea. Well, it was."

She led me to a small, well-furnished room. But something struck me as strange; it looked unlived in, there were no homely touches.

"Coffee?" she asked.

"Thank you."

She disappeared through a door and I looked around. My first impressions were strengthened, it was an anonymous space. A waiting room, rather than a living room. She came back with two large mugs of coffee.

"When did you get out?" I asked.

"Friday."

She'd rung me on Monday, asking if I wanted to meet the friend who made the films.

"Did you have someone to collect you?"

"No, I was fine."

"I'd have helped."

"I'm used to looking after myself; I don't let people get close easily."

The penny dropped.

"You don't live here," I said.

"God, no. This is – was – my business address."

"I get it. Nobody's visited my new place yet."

"Don't take it personally. I've learnt the hard way to keep my private life private."

"And Gina?"

"Dunno, she's out soon."

"Did you know her before?"

"No, but she knew me, apparently."

My puzzled expression made her laugh.

"Most places like this have a maid; a girl who does the appointments, meets the customers, runs the place. They all tend to know each other. She worked as a maid at a brothel which got turned over."

"I'm surprised she got sent down for that."

"I was too, but they were selling drugs, and they pinned that on Gina."

"How long's she in for?"

"Two years, but she's nearly done her time."

"Why did she attach herself to you?"

"She's submissive; I saw that as soon as I met her. She needs someone to own her. Her previous mistress at the brothel got ten years. She won't be seeing her for a long time, so she switched her loyalties to me."

"Are you taking her on?"

"I might. A little helper would be useful."

"And she is rather cute."

Kara broke into a wicked grin but said nothing.

"Tell me about Marco," I said.

"Don't know much about him personally. But he was a photographer who got into fetish stuff. Then he branched out into films. In everything he's done for me he's been professional and discreet. I've not worked for him, but he has done some photography for me."

"Is he the guy in the films?"

"No, I'm not sure who they are, but it's the same one or two men in all of them, I think."

The intercom buzzed again, and she went to answer it. A tall, skinny guy came through the door. He stood and looked at me, as if sizing me up. Crossing the room, he held out his hand.

"Hello, I'm Marco."

"Hi, I'm Bella."

We shook hands, and Kara went to make another coffee. He was still studying me, his eyes going from my hair to my body, peering at my face, then back to my hair.

"Kara was right," he said. "A distinctive look."

"That could be taken a number of ways," she replied, coming back with his coffee.

"I'm told you've done some spanking vids," he said.

"Yea, about half a dozen."

"With ... Dale?"

"Yea."

"So, all schoolgirls, with him playing headmaster."

"Yup."

"Up for something different?"

"That depends."

"On what?"

"On what you want me to do and how much you're offering."

He laughed.

"You've seen my work?"

"One of the Punished Pretties tapes."

"And ...?"

I told him what I thought of it, and we discussed whether I'd be prepared to do something similar. I was honest; I wasn't sure.

"How easily did you take the spankings?" he asked.

"They were fine; never felt much and never had any problems afterwards."

"It's always difficult to find girls who can take pain."

"So those who can are in short supply," Kara put in.

"Alright, Kara," Marco said. "Yes, that means they're at a premium."

He told me how he worked. He made roughly a film a month; they took three or four days to shoot. The girls in the one I'd seen would get around a thousand pounds. I hoped I'd hidden my surprise; it was a healthy fee.

"You must have a big market," I said.

"Yea, it's small here, but I have distributors on the continent. That's where most of the sales are."

After he'd answered all my questions, I said I'd think about it.

"Tell you what," he said. "I'm shooting next Tuesday. Why don't you come along and spend the day with us? I'm sure Rick and Cassie won't mind you watching."

"Cassie?"

"Yes, I pinched her from Dale. She got fed up with playing the schoolgirl, too."

I decided the opportunity was too good to miss and arranged to go to the filming. When he left, Kara came back and sat down.

"Any idea what you're going to do?" I asked her.

"I only know one thing; dammit, I only like one thing. I'm just going to have to be more careful."

"This doesn't look like a brothel," I said.

She gave me a withering look.

"It isn't."

"But I thought ..."

She put her mug on the table.

"Come with me," she said.

I followed her into a short corridor. At the end, she opened a door and turned on the lights. I looked slowly around, taking in the scene as realisation dawned. It was a dungeon. Deep red walls, with black metal furniture. Several pieces of equipment I didn't recognise, but Kara let me wander around and I soon worked out what they were for.

"You're a ..."

"I'm a dominatrix."

"So, what happened?"

"I've been doing it for a few years, and always worked alone. They can't touch you for that. But I let another girl use this place on the days I didn't work."

"They said you were working together."

"Exactly; it was my own stupid fault."

"What happened to her?"

"She ran away; no idea where she is."

"Bit ungrateful."

"Yea, but good luck to her."

"You're going to start up here again?"

"I doubt it. I need to find somewhere else and sneak below the radar for a bit."

"Let me guess, Sonny owns this place."

She smiled but said nothing.

"Is that how you know him?"

"Maybe."

"Okay, I'm not pushing. I find it's useful to know people's connections."

"It certainly is. It's also useful sometimes not to give them away."

She had a point.

"Is there a big demand for this?"

"Sure is. It's a small market, but a loyal one. I had a good group of regular clients and I need to find out if they're still mine."

When Cassie saw me, she came over and gave me a big hug. She was wearing a dressing gown and some fairly heavy make-up.

"Hi, Bella," she said. "I heard you got out. Are you okay?"

"Yea, not too bad."

"Marco said we had a voyeur, but he didn't say it was you."

"I didn't tell him I knew you. It could have been another Cassie."

"There's only one."

She introduced Rick, who was going to be hurting her today. He was a good-looking guy; tall and muscular, wearing leather trousers and a tight black t-shirt.

The rest of the day was a mixture of fascination and frustration. Marco worked one camera and his assistant, Andy, worked another. But it was still all start and stop, as they moved positions to get different angles and asked Rick and Cassie to repeat things to get the right shots.

It wasn't exactly erotic, but I couldn't take my eyes off some of the action. I felt that same thrill as the belt or the cane landed on Cassie's bare flesh. Rick knew what he was doing and never let his own urges take over. By the end of filming, her bum and thighs were red, verging on purple, and she'd had at least three orgasms.

Rick calmly put a leather jacket on, nodded to us and left.

"He was a calm one," I said as Cassie carefully put some loose clothes on. The occasional grimace told me the pain was real.

"He's gay," she said.

"Ah, that explains a lot."

94

"Still, he knows what he's doing," she added, with a wink.
"What's it like?" I asked.
"Not bad. It hurts, but you know I can handle pain."
"Compared to a spanking?"
"A whole different level. You going to try it?"
"I reckon so. I need to make some money."
"Everything else come to an end?"
"Yea, Gordon's retired, and Dale's stuff is boring."
"Tell me about it, the same thing every time. At least these are different and the money's better too."
Marco came over.
"Okay, Cas?"
"Yea. Was it alright?"
"You two work well together. It'll be good."
He handed her a thick envelope which she shoved into her bag.
"Well, Bella. What did you think?"
"It was what I imagined. Stop, start, stop, start."
"That's film-making."
"Plus, a purple ass."
Cassie laughed.
"Nothing ever changes, does it?" she said.
"Going to become my next star?" he asked.
"I'll think about it."
I left with Cassie and we caught the tube back into the city. I asked her about the work, and her answers told me Marco had been up-front about everything.
"How long will those marks take to go?" I asked her.
"About a week."
"And they go completely?"
"Yea. He uses guys who know what they're doing. I've never had a problem."
"Does Della do it, as well?"
"She's done one or two, but she can't deal with as much pain. She's doing the odd porn film now."
When I got home, I made something to eat and thought about what I'd seen. If Cassie could take it, so could I. I

didn't want to go down the porn route. I had other options. I could go back to the sex work, but I'd had enough of that. The chances of finding another set-up like Gordon's was slim and I knew I'd been lucky. I'd got through it without being assaulted or catching anything. I wanted it to stay that way.

I could leave it all behind and find a proper job. But my skills were limited and the thought of going to work every day for much less than I'd been earning didn't appeal. I liked the freedom the sex work had given me. Money and plenty of time to enjoy it. I needed something that gave me the same independence.

"Come in," Kara said. "Be careful what you touch." She was covered in paint.

"Thanks."

She'd invited me to see her new set-up. It was in an old mews building in Whitechapel and was remarkably untouched. The ground floor had been converted into a living space, with heat and light, but a lot of the original fittings had been left, including the stall divides.

"This is some place," I said.

"Isn't it?"

"Sonny?"

She shrugged.

"Going to keep the stalls?" I asked.

"Yea. I think so. They're all on hinges, so you can swing them out of the way if you want to. Just needs tarting up. Come on, I'll take a break."

She covered the pot of paint, put her brush down and went over to a doorway.

"Coffee for two," she called out and came back to me, pointing out a couple of canvas chairs. She saw my curiosity at the instruction but said nothing.

"There's another room upstairs I'm doing up as well in a more conventional style, but this will be good when I've finished."

I heard footsteps on the stairs and wasn't surprised when Gina appeared, carrying a tray with two mugs and some biscuits.

"Hi, Gina," I said.

She looked at Kara for instructions; a gentle nod gave permission.

"Hello, Bella. It's good to see you."

"You too. Glad to be out?"

"Yes, thank you."

"Take a break, Gina. Then try and finish that room."

"Yes, ma'am. Thank you."

She went back up the stairs.

"Willing little helper?" I said.

"She's good. Still needs a little training. She's very diffident but surprisingly competent."

"Competent at what?"

Kara saw my smile.

"Lots of things," was all she said, returning the smile.

She gave me a quick tour of the building and what she planned to do. It was quite a place; lots of old touches and plenty of beams and rings on the wall. I wouldn't have noticed them unless Kara had told me how she planned to use them. It was an eye-opener into her world.

"Going to do it?" she asked after I told her about my experience watching the filming.

"I'll give it a go. The money's good and I seem to be able to take pain quite well."

"We'll see," she replied, a knowing smile on her face.

Chapter 14 - A Step Up

"This is Troy," Marco said, introducing me to the man who was going to be the instrument of my pain.

"Hello, Bella," Troy said.

I returned the greeting as we shook hands. He was a good-looking guy of about thirty; tall, well-built, with long dark hair, tied back in a ponytail. He was wearing what seemed to be the uniform for these films; leather trousers and a tight black top.

"Troy's done a lot of these," Marco said. "So, he knows what he's doing."

He wandered off to get the cameras and lights set-up, leaving me with Troy.

"Your first time?" he asked.

"Yes. Well, I've done a few spanking films, but nothing else."

"Were you okay with that?"

"Yea, didn't give me any problems."

Marco had sent me a rough plan we were going to follow. It wasn't a script; I didn't have to say anything, and Troy was presumably going to keep his lines to a minimum as well. The sound of implements hitting skin and my moans and groans were what mattered.

The set was one of those I'd seen in the film I'd watched; a modern take on a dungeon. A couple of padded benches, a flogging horse and a rope suspended from the ceiling. The look was finished off with some painted backdrops, room dividers and, bizarrely, two huge potted plants.

Marco and Andy, his cameraman, came over and we sat down to run through the plan. It was all straightforward; unlike a lot of filming, we had to shoot it in order, otherwise, the colour of my skin would change in the wrong places.

"Everybody ready?" Marco asked. There were no dissenting voices. "Let's go."

We went over to the set and I took off my gown. Troy tied my wrists to the hanging rope and left me.

"Right, Bella," Marco said. "Look nervous, frightened. You've been brought here, stripped, tied up. You don't know what's happening."

I tried; it wasn't easy. I wasn't an actor, but I did my best. A lot of looking around, wriggling, trying to free myself. Unfortunately, I was too good and dropped to the floor as my hands slipped through the rope.

"Stop," Marco said, as I burst out laughing, swiftly followed by Andy and Troy, who came over to tie me up again. He pulled the rope a couple of times to make sure it would hold me this time.

After a few more minutes of pretend struggling, a door in one side opened and Troy came in. I stopped moving. He was wearing a full head mask, with holes for his eyes and mouth, his ponytail hanging down the back. It was an intimidating look. I watched him as he walked painfully slowly towards me and continued around me. I turned to follow him, but he grabbed my hair and pulled my head towards him.

"Stand still," he said in a deep voice. "You only move when I tell you."

He pushed me away and I stood stock-still as he circled me several times, finally letting his hand run over my body. He stopped behind me and squeezed my bum with one hand, clamping the other over my breast and pinching the nipple. I could hear his breathing by my ear. He was a lot calmer than me, and I realised my tension wasn't good acting; it was real.

I wasn't sure if it was anxiety about this performance or if the situation was actually working for me.

Troy came around to face me, and bent me forward under his arm, putting it around my waist, holding me tight. We were facing opposite directions and I couldn't see what was happening. I soon found out as his hand came down on my bum. I jumped at the first strike, but he started softly, and I soon settled. He was moving the impact point around and it wasn't hurting.

"Stop," Marco said. "Bella, you may be able to take this, but I need you to react more. You're not making a sound."

"Sorry."

"It's okay, but remember you're supposed to be a terrified innocent."

We started again, and I made some appropriate noises. At one point, I gave a squeak at the wrong moment and burst into a fit of the giggles.

"Stop," Marco said again, in a slightly frustrated voice.

"Sorry. I'm not used to faking it."

Even Marco laughed at that. We resumed and got a long section completed. Troy spanked me harder and moved me around a few times. Then he let me go again, and stood in front of me, running a hand over my torso, my breasts, ending between my legs. As his hand landed over my pussy, I was surprised at my reaction. I gasped as a wave of pleasure swept through me and my body pressed towards his touch.

He slid his hand over my groin a few times and I moaned; wanting more. There was no doubt this was turning me on. But I was here to act, and pleasure would be given when Marco decided it was needed.

Troy went over to a table and picked up a flogger. I watched this masked figure as he flailed it through the air a few times; this was the real test. The stakes were about to be raised.

He came across to me and lifted the flogger above me, allowed it to trail over my skin.

"React," Marco said quietly. I did as I was instructed, but it was difficult. This was all new to me and I was more interested in finding out how it felt than I was about performing for the camera.

Troy began to twirl the fronds, allowing them to stroke my skin. He started gently and I let my brain take in the sensations; like wandering naked through soft undergrowth. My mind was beginning to enjoy the feeling when it was woken by a stinging pulse. Troy was using the flogger in anger. Circling my body, landing the leather in a different place every time; my breasts, my tummy, my thighs, my back.

I was reacting naturally now, my body flinching from the contact. But it wasn't painful; I could feel the sting, followed by a burning, but it didn't hurt. I savoured these new sensations.

Troy was striking with more force, repeating strokes on the same area a few times before moving on. Even using it between my legs; I opened them, wanting the contact.

"Close them," Marco barked; I obeyed.

I closed my eyes and let the blows fall, concentrating on the feeling. It wasn't unpleasant and my mind began to wander.

"Stop," Marco said, and I turned to see him frowning at me. "You're not supposed to be enjoying it, Bella." Andy laughed.

"Sorry."

"Enjoy it all you want, but please at least look as if you're not."

This time, I made more noise and reacted to each stroke. Troy turned his attention to my bum and increased the force. This time, I didn't need to act; the sting was strong, and I let my body twist and turn on the rope as he hit. Marco stopped us, adjusted our position, and put one of the cameras in front of me.

"I want facial expressions, Bella."

Troy continued and I let go, not trying to hide my reactions.

"Look at the camera."

I stared into the lens and tried to exaggerate my response.

"Natural," Marco said.

"Make ... up ... your ... bloody ... mind," I said between strokes, and this time, Troy laughed.

"Stop," Marco said, but at least he was smiling, too. "Take a break."

We sat on the floor while Andy made some tea. The room wasn't very warm, though I don't think that was the reason my nipples were hard. It was a strange experience. We were doing something that would be very erotic under other circumstances. I was definitely responding to it.

But this was a job. Not like the parties, though. At those, I knew I was going to get fucked, and sometimes would enjoy it. Here, everything was to order. As we drank tea, my body relaxed, and the desire slipped away.

"Okay?" Marco asked.

"Fine."

"Good. You're doing well. Let's crack on."

Troy tied me up again, but as soon as the camera rolled, he untied me and took me over to the horse. He laid my shoulders on it and stretched my arms out, tying one to each end. My bum was sticking out behind me, feeling very vulnerable. He ran his hand over my cheeks and let them slip between my legs. I opened them a little to give him access and I smiled as I heard Marco groan.

Troy played the flogger over my bum a few times before bringing it down hard, making me jump. As he continued, my hips squirmed under the onslaught. Again, Andy was filming my face, capturing my expressions. They were real enough this time.

It stopped suddenly and I let myself relax and draw breath. Troy came around and bent in front of me.

"Okay?"

"Yea," I replied.

"Not bad for a beginner," he grinned. "It's time for this."

He was holding a cane; about three feet long. It looked so harmless, but it was this I'd been most fearful of. The cameras were repositioned, and we began the scene. Troy stood behind me to one side and tapped the cane against my cheeks.

I felt my whole body tense and tried to prepare for the first stroke. It came before I was ready, and I cried out as it bit into my skin. My whole body trembled as first an intense stinging spread out from the impact, then a dull pain followed, much more slowly.

Another stroke followed, then another. I was yelping with each bite, my legs buckling slightly. Each time they did, Troy stopped and slipped his hand between my legs. I needed that touch; it brought me back to the present and my legs straightened.

I have no idea how many strokes he gave me; a lot more than the proverbial six. Many more. At one point, the flurry increased, and I squealed at the continuous stinging, my legs buckling and my body struggling to stay still. I suddenly felt his hand between my legs.

No gentle touch this time; I gasped as his fingers invaded me and he fucked me with them. He knew what he was doing and before long, an intense orgasm flooded over me, my legs giving way this time. He followed me down, his fingers extending my climax as I knelt by the horse, still roped to it.

He slid them out and gave my bum a few slaps; the pain as he slapped my cane welts reigniting my dying orgasm one last time. I let myself relax; the position was uncomfortable, but the room was silent as I came down. Finally, Marco spoke.

"Okay."

Troy untied my arms and I slumped to the floor. He bent by me.

"That was something else. Are you okay?"

"Yea. Fine."

"Let's have some lunch," Marco said. Troy took the mask off and went to get my gown, laying it over my shoulders. After a few minutes, I put it on and went over to join them. The sandwiches were from a garage by the look of things, but after the first bite, I didn't care. I was hungry and munched into them. After a few bites, I looked up to see the three guys smiling at me.

"What?"

"Hungry?" Marco said.

"Mmm."

"Hurting?" Troy asked.

I thought about it, surprised I hadn't noticed it. Before today, I'd tried to imagine what a caning would be like; how it would feel. But I'd got up, walked, and sat on a chair without even thinking about it.

"Not much," I said. "Stings, though." I could feel my bum was hot and if I wriggled on the chair, the pain made me flinch. But it wasn't anything like I'd expected. They looked at each other and back at me.

"What?" I said again.

"I think you may have found a new career," Troy said.

We finished eating and sat around for half an hour chatting.

"If you're okay, I want to change the plan a bit," Marco said and told us what he wanted. It sounded easy enough.

Troy tied me to one of the benches on my back, tying my arms above my head. Then he lifted my legs, bent them, and tied them wide apart. I felt vulnerable again, my sex open and exposed.

He appeared in front of me with a riding crop and for the next ten minutes, he used it lightly all over my body. It was an interesting sensation; a brief sting leaving a warm patch on my skin. It got more interesting as he concentrated on my inner thighs, moving nearer to my pussy. In between strikes, he let the leather end run over my clit, sometimes lightly, sometimes with a firmer touch. I was enjoying the experience.

He knelt to one side and let his fingers run over it and I moaned as he slid them into me, his thumb rubbing my bud. I closed my eyes allowing the pleasure to spread through me but opened them wide when the crop landed heavily on my thighs again.

His fingers began to fuck me, and I knew my climax wouldn't be long. When it came, he didn't stop. Roughly driving into me, he used the crop on my breasts. My body struggled to writhe, both from the pleasure between my legs and the pain on my breasts, but I was tied tightly and couldn't move.

My climax hadn't waned before it overtook me again. Still, he continued. I was panting now, overwhelmed by the situation. Helpless under the onslaught. I heard myself scream as a third orgasm ripped through me. My whole body was shaking now, my throat emitting a series of garbled sounds. I was dimly aware of Troy laying the crop between my legs and walking away.

The next thing I remember was my gown being laid over me as the bindings were undone. I slowly stretched my limbs as they came back to life. Troy was sitting on the end of the bench.

"Okay?" he asked.

"Yea. Stiff."

"Me too." He was grinning and it took me a moment to pick up the innuendo.

"You're not gay?"

"Nope."

"How do you cope with doing this?"

"My girlfriend is always ready and waiting when I get home after one of these."

"Lucky her."

"You're single?"

"Yea. I don't seem to have much luck with partners."

Troy and I went into a side room to get changed. He was right, his partner was in for a good time when he got home. I looked at his cock; quite something to behold, even now. He smiled when he saw me, and I looked away.

"Find yourself a guy," he said. "You're quite something."

"Might fancy a girl," I replied.

"Okay, find a girl."

"Can't seem to find either at the moment."

I did notice the results of the day as I dressed, silently cursing I hadn't worn looser clothes. When we went back to Marco and Andy, they were packing up.

"Might need you to dub some sounds," Marco said. "I'll let you know."

He handed Troy and me an envelope each and we all departed. I spent half an hour soaking in a warm bath when I got home and carefully rubbed moisturiser over my whole body. When I went to bed, I wondered what the fuss was about. I ached, but it wasn't severe.

When I woke up in the morning, my bum hurt like hell and I could hardly move.

Chapter 15 - Gina's Balm

"You look a bit delicate," Kara said, a big grin on her face. "Come in."

"Just a little. Thanks"

"You're walking like you've messed yourself."

I'd promised I'd go and see her the next day to let her know how I got on. I put on a loose dress and only a thong to avoid rubbing the marks.

"How did it go?" she asked.

We were sitting on a velvet chaise longue in the stable room. She'd made remarkable progress and the room looked fabulous. Fully decorated with large rugs covering the stone floor. She and Gina were adding the finishing touches and there was a stack of framed pictures leaning against one wall waiting to be hung.

"It wasn't as bad as I feared."

She insisted on a blow by blow account of the filming and listened intently as I described the action. She occasionally glanced at Gina who was kneeling by her side, listening as keenly as her mistress.

"Sounds like you enjoyed it," Kara said as I finished.

"Can't deny it had an effect."

"Perhaps I should have taken you on rather than this little one."

Gina pouted and her mistress stroked her hair in reassurance.

"Don't see myself as anyone's submissive," I replied. "No offence, Gina."

Gina smiled and gave a gentle nod.

"No, I guess not," Kara replied, giving me a sultry smile. "Pity."

"One not enough for you?" I asked, returning it.

"I think I could handle the two of you."

There was a pause in the conversation as we all took in the unsaid implications of the exchange.

"So," Kara said. "How's your bum?"

"It's hurting this morning. It was fine last night."

"Let's have a look," she said.

I hesitated briefly, but she'd watched me masturbate in prison; I had no more to hide. I stood, turned around and lifted my dress. A short silence was followed by a chuckle.

"Well, girl. If that was your first time, you can be proud. That's impressive. Come closer."

I shuffled backwards and as I reached her, I winced as she gently ran her fingers over my skin and explored the bruises and welts. We both knew she carried on far longer than necessary, her fingers running between my thighs and down my legs before coming back to rest on my bum.

"What do you think, Gina?" she said.

"It needs the right treatment, mistress."

"Exactly what I was thinking."

Gina got up and went upstairs as I dropped my dress and turned around.

"Dress off," Kara said, and I pulled it over my head. I was naked apart from the thong, as my breasts were still sore, and I didn't fancy the tightness of a bra. Kara made no attempt to hide her gaze as her eyes wandered over my body. I stood there with mixed feelings. I liked Kara; we had become friends easily. And I was attracted to her physically, but something was holding me back from pursuing that interest and I wasn't sure what. I wondered what she was thinking.

Gina returned with a couple of towels and a glass bottle. She put the towels over the cushions of a sofa and looked at me expectantly.

"Lie down, Bella," Kara said. "Let Gina take care of you. She's normally the recipient, it'll make a change."

I made myself comfortable on my front and laid my arms above my head. Gina shook the bottle and poured some of the thick contents onto her hand. I tensed as the lotion touched my skin and she began to massage it in. Its coolness had an immediate soothing effect, and my body relaxed, giving in to the touch of her fingers. She applied the lotion generously and rubbed it gently into my bum and thighs. It seemed to have a numbing effect and the pain eased.

I turned my head to look at Kara. She was watching her sub massaging my nearly naked body with a faint smile on her face.

"What is this stuff?" I asked her.

"Something I put together myself. A good moisturiser with aloe and arnica mixed in."

"Does it work?"

"I wouldn't know," she replied with a grin. "I'm never on the receiving end. You'd better ask Gina."

"Gina?"

"Yes, it's good. It feels cool and makes me recover more quickly."

"Which means," Kara said, "she's ready for me again."

I wondered how often Gina was on the receiving end of Kara's discipline and if their needs coincided. I didn't yet understand this sort of relationship.

"Does Gina need correction often?" I asked.

"From time to time," Kara replied. "Don't you, Gina?"

"Yes, ma'am."

"But she's a good girl most of the time."

"Thank you, ma'am."

"So then, we do it for fun."

That was the part I couldn't work out. I'd taken the spankings without a problem, and now the more severe treatment was tolerable. But I'd done it for money. It hadn't been terrible and parts of it had turned me on, but I couldn't imagine it forming a part of a private relationship.

I looked back at Gina, still massaging my body. I noticed a dreamy look on her face and realised she was enjoying it. The heat between my legs told me I was, as well.

"She's good, isn't she?" Kara asked.

"Mmm. It's definitely helping," I replied, trying to ignore the increasing pleasure.

"Why don't you turn over?"

I rolled over and lowered myself back onto the towels. I noticed how hard my nipples were, with a mix of pain and pleasure. They'd been struck by the flogger and crop and had a few sore patches. Gina poured some of the lotion onto my tummy and smoothed it out over my skin.

My mind was wandering, wondering how far this was going; how far I wanted it to go. I watched Gina, but she didn't meet my eye. She was looking at what she was doing, which was delicately running her greased fingers around my nipples, an engrossed expression on her face.

I closed my eyes and left her to it. Her touch was perfect; firm enough to stir me, but gentle enough to avoid inflaming the sore areas. I hadn't had sex for pleasure since Fran left and I missed it. This was getting serious. Her hands left my breasts and worked over my tummy to my thighs. They had received the crop's treatment when I'd been tied up, and those marks went all the way to my pussy. Where would Gina stop?

As her fingers worked their way down between my thighs, I opened my legs without thinking and she moved closer to the edges of my thong. But they didn't stop, pushing the edges aside to reach the skin under them. Very close to my sex.

"Bella may not want you to go there, Gina," Kara said. The fingers moved away, and I felt a wave of frustration; it must have shown. "Or do you?" she added. I looked at her, that same smile still on her face, challenging me. "She will if you want, won't you, Gina?"

"Yes, ma'am. Willingly."

I looked at Kara, then at Gina, both of them watching me closely. I thought for a moment before reaching down and sliding my thong off. As I relaxed again, Gina's fingers returned to my inner thighs and worked in small circles, moving towards my sex again.

When they slid either side of my labia, a wave of warm shivers washed over my groin and my tummy, ending in a long sigh. Before I'd drawn breath again, her fingers were delicately gliding over my pussy lips, and my legs were spreading further. Just as her fingers were moving to the most sensitive areas, she stopped. I looked up, and Gina was looking at Kara. I followed her gaze in time to see Kara smile and nod.

Before I picked up the meaning, Gina turned back and her fingers returned to my pussy, but with real intent this time. She ran them over my flesh, letting them continue over my clit, making my body flinch. One hand rested low on my thigh, its fingers gently massaging the area below my pussy, occasionally straying to the softer flesh above. The other was spreading me, with a finger or two circling my entrance.

Gina was wearing a loose dress and I couldn't resist reaching out to touch her leg, but an alarm bell in my head stopped me and I looked over at Kara, not wanting to offend her. She smiled.

"Gina," she said softly. "I think Bella would like to see more of you."

"Yes, ma'am," Gina replied and straightened. In one move, she lifted her dress over her head, revealing her nakedness underneath. She bent over me again, and I let my hand land on her thigh and wander to her bum. I'd seen her naked in prison and she was cute; stroking her bare bum was no hardship.

She dropped her head, and I gasped as her tongue lapped across my entrance, my legs tensing at the shock. My hand squeezed her bum hard and she gave a little bleat under the pressure. I released my grip as her tongue pushed into me, her lips enclosing my labia.

"Don't be afraid to hurt her," Kara said. I'd almost forgotten her presence and when I looked over to her, she'd removed most of her clothes and was laying back, her legs apart, masturbating while she watched us.

It was all a little surreal. Gina was licking and sucking my pussy, I had my hand on her bum, and was watching Kara play with herself. I let my hand slide between Gina's legs and her head came up sharply as I found her sex and slid my fingers over it, surprised by how wet she was.

I let my thumb slide into her, and rested two fingers either side of her clit, gently rocking them from side to side. It was too much, and her head dropped onto my groin, her breath coming in shallow, rapid bursts. I pressed more firmly, and her hips slowly rose until she gave a few sweet chirps as her climax came, those hips jerking a few times before stilling again.

After a few moments of silence, she looked at me, smiled and lowered her head onto me again. I felt her lips surround my hood and her tongue began to flick my clit. It didn't take long; my thumb and finger tensed and gripped her sensitive flesh between them as she took me to orgasm. An intense, rippling orgasm, increased by looking at Kara who was also reaching her peak and groaning loudly. We held each other's gaze for a few seconds before relaxing into our own reverie.

In the silence that followed, all I could hear was the breathing of three satisfied women.

"A touch of déjà vu, I think," Kara said. It was a reverse of our first meeting. Gina was resting her head on my groin and I realised I was slowly stroking her hair. I looked down and saw her staring back, a look of complete contentment on her face.

"Be careful, Bella," Kara said. "She'll be purring in a minute. Have you said thank you, Gina?"

"No, ma'am. Thank you, Bella."

"Thank you," I replied, then turned to Kara. "Or should I thank you? I don't know the etiquette here."

"I'm happy for Gina to get the credit. I told you, she's a good girl most of the time."

As she lifted herself off me, Gina looked like the cat who got the cream; she was beaming.

"Thank you, ma'am."

"Staying for lunch?" Kara asked me.

"If it's no trouble."

"No trouble for me," she replied. "Gina, can you rustle up something?"

"Certainly, ma'am."

Gina picked up her dress and disappeared upstairs.

"Feeling better?" Kara asked.

"I must be, I haven't even thought about the pain. But now you mention it ..."

"The mind is a powerful thing, particularly where pain is concerned. Get that in the right place, and you can cope with almost anything."

It was a piece of advice that was to become important to me over the coming years.

"And it's a good idea to be fit, as well."

She bullied me into joining the gym she went to. I'd seen the benefits briefly when I'd been inside. I was never an addict, but I found that a good workout worked wonders for body and soul.

Chapter 16 - An Idea

When I saw the final version of the film, I was impressed. By my performance, yes, but also by the quality of the film and the packaging. It was so much better than Dale's product. Troy and I had to go in to do a few overdubs; in my case, just a load of moans, groans, and screams.

It had been hilarious, trying to match the sounds to my movements and I'd found myself on the wrong end of Marco's frustration again, if only mildly. Marco and Andy worked well together. Marco was the creative mind in control of how the finished product looked. He had a clear view of what the customers wanted and did his best to produce it.

Andy was the technical controller. He was a whizz with the lighting and cameras and proved an excellent editor and looked after the copying and distribution.

They had a small cadre of performers they used; five women and five men. I met and performed with all the guys over the next few months. I only met a couple of the women, as Marco filmed one scene at a time, and I never worked with the other girls.

Although I say it myself, I proved popular. Marco took feedback seriously and asked his European distributors to get as much as he could. My films became the best-sellers in his range and ideas came in from customers about what they'd like to see me endure. A few were far too extreme; some were weird. But some cropped up again and again and we incorporated them in our scenes.

"So," Kara said. "You're a film star now."

"Not quite, but it seems to be going well."

I'd lent her copies of my two first films.

"What's next?"

"How do you mean?"

"Well, you know what happened with the spanking guy. It gets repetitive; the customers get bored and want someone or something new. And you'll get bored, too."

I knew she was right. I was happy doing the work for now. It wasn't difficult and it paid well. But there were only so many scenarios, so many positions, so many punishments. Then all you could do was go back to the beginning and start again.

"I don't know. I'll worry about that when it happens."

I was spending the evening with her and Gina. For once, Gina hadn't had to cook; we had a takeaway.

Kara was back up and running now. Most of her old clients had come back and she'd attracted a few more.

"Where do they come from?" I asked.

"It's all word of mouth. Guys who want my services are part of a small group; they often know each other or belong to some half-secret club. If you're good, word gets around."

"No female clients?"

"I've had one or two in the past, but they're rare."

"Women don't want it?"

"Oh, they do. More than people think." She looked at Gina and they shared a knowing look. "But most women are too shy to pay for it."

"Do all the men want the same thing?"

"Oh, God, no. Everyone's different. Some want a good thrashing; others want to be humiliated. You think of it, someone will want it. I'll do anything they want, within my own rules."

I summoned up the courage to ask the question I'd wanted to ask all along.

"Do they all want sex?"

She chuckled.

"You mean, do I fuck them all?"

"Well …"

"No, I don't. Many of them aren't after that, anyway. I'm very choosy and only accept new people after we've met and talked. Some I turn away straightaway."

"Too extreme?"

"Sometimes, but I may just have a bad feeling about them. There are plenty of rotten apples out there."

"Yea, I've met a few."

"Others, I'll take on a trial basis. I have a few long-standing clients where sex is involved, but they're in the minority."

"Is it … profitable?"

"I wouldn't do it, otherwise."

"Much competition?"

She rolled her eyes and gave a hollow laugh.

"There are lots of women calling themselves dominatrices. Most are wannabes; they dress in something black, wave a riding crop in the air and call themselves mistresses. Then they wonder why they only ever see guys once. Why they keep on having to accommodate a steady stream of new clients, increasing their risk."

"Okay, why?"

"Because they don't know what they're doing. They think it's all about bossing men around. There's a hell of a lot more to it than that. The men who seek out people like me know what they want; it may have taken them years to summon up the courage. And it's not some twenty-year-old prancing around in a cheap pair of boots and watching the clock. I've got a small group of regular clients who pay me well because I give them what they want."

"Makes sense."

"Why, thinking of trying it?"

"No, taking punishment seems to be my forte."

"You won't know if you don't try it."

"No, but how do you do that? How did you get started?"

"Being in the right place at the right time."

"What happened?"

"I knew I was the dominant partner long before I even considered making a living out of it. Right from my teens, I enjoyed being in charge. I was always the boss.

"That's unusual, surely?"

"I guess it is, but I didn't know it at the time. I was lucky enough to meet someone who matched my needs when I was still young. I learnt a hell of a lot with him."

"How did it become a living?"

"That was later. I did all sorts of ordinary jobs, but he was in a small group of like-minded people and I joined them. A few were involved in the sex industry in one way or another. When I was made redundant from another boring office job, one of the women who worked as a Domme half-jokingly suggested I tried it. I took her at her word, and she took me under her wing. The rest, as they say, is history."

"Hope you don't mind me asking."

"I'm not ashamed of what I do; I love it. Professionally and personally. I don't shout about it, but I'll talk to people I trust."

"Thank you," I said, genuinely flattered. "What about the girls?"

"That was an accident, too. I got friendly with a girl in the group who was submissive, and she asked if I topped women. I hadn't done anything with another woman, but I agreed to try it. Turned out she fancied me, and one thing led to another. We were together for a few years and I haven't looked back since."

"So, professionally you work with men ..."

"... and personally, prefer a woman."

"Not sure I could give up men completely."

"You don't have to; do what you want. Gives you more choice."

I wanted to ask Gina about her background, but it seemed impolite, so left it at that. Gina rolled some joints and we chilled. I didn't smoke them much now. My days of drug-taking were over; they reminded me too much of the past. Of Carla, and then of Fran. I was over her but didn't always want those memories.

As we relaxed, we told each other stories of our past; most of them salacious. Kara had some tales to tell, mostly about previous clients. It was quite an eye-opener. I suppose I thought it would be like the things I did in my films, only with the roles reversed. But a lot of it wasn't. There were fetishes and fantasies I hadn't even dreamed of; several I struggled to make sense of, even after Kara described them.

"Does anything shock you?" I asked.

"Not really," she replied. "Not anymore. I've heard it all, although I still get the occasional odd request. I'm very clear about what I will do and what I won't."

"Do you enjoy it?"

She didn't reply immediately, and I saw she was considering the question. It seemed strange at first, but I guess it was a job. How many people think about whether they enjoy their job?

"Yes, I do. But not in the way you might have meant the question. I'm a controller; I like to be in charge. So, they get what they want, whatever it may be, and I get to indulge my need to control. It's a perfect role for me."

"Does it get you off?"

"Sometimes. When the person, the activity and the timing are all right, it can be intensely satisfying. But you know what it's like; sometimes, you're not in the mood, but still have to perform."

"Yea, I know that feeling."

"At the end of the day, it's my job. I don't always feel like it, but that's when it's all about being professional. The client shouldn't be able to see what mood I'm in from one session to the next. But overall, I couldn't imagine doing anything else."

"Ever had any trouble?"

"Once or twice in the early days when I was less careful. But I can look after myself now."

I'd seen her naked; she had a beautiful body, but it was lean and muscular.

"The gym work?"

"Partly, but mainly Judo."

"Judo?"

"Yea. One of my clients years ago was into it and suggested I try it."

"Do you still do it?"

"Every week; Gina's learning now so we can practice together. Why not come along?"

I'd found another passion.

"We're doing well enough with what we're doing," Marco said.

"Yea, but how about adding some variety?" I replied.

At the end of filming, I'd cornered him and asked if he'd thought about expanding his set-up.

"Such as?"

"How about adding a second girl?"

"Still with one guy?"

"Yea, or the second girl is a top, as well."

"Not interested in working with female tops. I've had some bad experiences."

I wondered what they were but didn't feel it was an appropriate time to ask.

"Okay, but why not try with two girls getting punished?"

"I'll think about it."

Kara had been right; I was getting bored. We were doing the same things again and again. I was getting well rewarded but needed something else. If Marco wasn't going to produce other things, perhaps I should think about it myself.

"I've never considered it," Kara said.

"Would you?" I replied.

"I'm quite private; not sure I want the world to see what I do."

I'd asked her if she would be prepared to make a film or two.

"Anyway," she said. "If Marco's not interested, it's not going to happen."

"Don't be so sure."

"What are you up to?"

"How would it be if I made my own films?"

She screwed her eyes up and studied me.

"You're seriously considering this, aren't you?"

"Why not?"

"It'll be a lot of work. And need a lot of money to set up."

"I know."

"Why don't you ask Marco if he'll let you do your own thing under his umbrella?"

"Because I like to run things my way."

She laughed.

"We'll make a Domme of you, yet."

I hadn't convinced Marco to do new things, and I hadn't persuaded Kara to be my first star. But the more I thought about it, the more the idea appealed. I'd done enough films now to understand the basic requirements. Lighting, cameras, an editing suite, and someone who knew how to use them. A good set or two and some good-looking performers.

The problem was how to get the films distributed. So, I sat Marco down and explained my plan. He was cynical.

"You don't know anything about the business," he said.

"I know it from in front of the camera. Come on, Marco, there's not much to making the films. It's everything else I need help with, particularly distribution."

"That's the bit that took me an age to develop."

"So how about sharing?"

He looked at me suspiciously.

"Sharing?"

"Yea. I make the films you don't want to, and you introduce me to your distributors."

"Why would I do that? What's in it for me?"

"We could discuss that."

I could see that piqued his interest.

"Where will you get the equipment?" he asked. "And no, you can't borrow mine."

"Forget that for a moment. If I can come up with a product, are you prepared to help with distribution for the right price?"

I'd caught him unprepared and he was racing to catch up.

"Why not? This is a tough business, Bella. You'll never get this off the ground."

Chapter 17 - Swapping Roles

I spent a lot of time picking Kara's brain. What did her clients ask for? What did they like? What were the popular scenarios and fantasies? I visited sex shops and studied what was on offer. There were plenty of traditional spanking films, the sort I'd made with Dale. Then there were the type I made for Marco; I found a few of my films on the shelves.

But there weren't many featuring female domination; just a few, mainly from Germany. Was this because, as Marco insisted, there wasn't a market? Or was it because nobody was meeting the need? I spent a few weeks thinking about it; I had the money salted away to set this up and no-one else was aware of that. But it was there to secure my future, so I had to be sure this would be a good move.

I borrowed Andy for a day to find out what I would need. He took me to see a friend of his who supplied professional video equipment.

"It would be a hell of an investment, Bella," Andy said. "How would you find the money?"

"Leave that to me. What about high definition?"

"Don't bother with that, it might not take off," he replied.

"That's where you're wrong," Nigel, his salesman friend said. "I reckon DVDs will take over from VHS."

"It could be another fad."

"Is Marco switching?" I asked.

"Not on your life," Andy replied.

"Have you suggested it?"

"Yea. He's not interested."

That was enough for me. I'd decided Marco was too stuck in his ways. If he wasn't going to switch up, I would. By the end of the day, I had a shopping list. It was long, complex, very expensive and would take a big chunk out of my investments. I needed to be sure it was worth it.

"Are you going to do it?" Kara asked.

"I'm prepared to, but what I need now is the people."

"Who?"

"I need someone to operate the cameras and do the editing. And I need performers."

"Can't you ask the people who do films for Marco?"

"The girls, possibly, although it'll piss him off. But I need at least one Domme and a submissive guy. Any ideas?"

She looked pensive and didn't reply for a while, before turning to Gina.

"Know anyone?" she asked.

Gina blushed but looked thoughtful.

"She's got her own little network," Kara said. "She's more connected than I am."

"I know a guy who might do it," Gina said. "He's a sub and a bit of an exhibitionist, but whether he'll want to do it on camera ..."

"Know him well enough to ask?"

"Yea, I think so."

"Thanks, Gina," I said, turning to Kara. "All I need now is the star."

I held her gaze and, eventually, she chuckled.

"I'm not sure," she said. "Why don't you do it?"

"Kara, I've always been on the receiving end. I wouldn't know what the hell to do. I need someone who looks the part and acts the part."

"I could teach you."

"How long did it take you to feel comfortable in this skin?"

"About five years."

"Exactly."

"But you're doing it on film. You're acting. You can stop and re-shoot it."

"Yea. But it still needs to feel right."

"Are you prepared to try?"

I studied her; she was serious.

"I guess so," I replied.

"In that case, I'll make you a deal. I'll coach you. If – and I mean if – you can't do it, I'll make you one of your damn films. Deal?"

"Yea, deal. Thanks."

"We'd better get started."

"How?"

Kara looked at Gina, who returned a gorgeous smile, full of anticipation.

"Gina has some minus points to wipe off this week. I think you ought to carry out her punishment."

I was caught by surprise. I looked at Gina and she was sitting on the edge of her chair, her hands on her knees, raring to go. She was looking at me as if I was the answer to her prayers and I didn't have a clue what to do.

"Well, come on teacher," I said to Kara. "Help me out here."

"I'll coach you, but I'm not going to make you a copy of me. You need to find your own persona. We'll start with something simple; give Gina a spanking."

I took a deep breath and trawled through my memory. I'd been spanked dozens of times, but I went back to the performances Fran and I had done. Watching her being spanked had been a turn on for me; that would have to be my template.

"Gina ..."

"Yes ... Miss Bella."

The respectful moniker made me smile; she was a quick thinker.

"Come here."

She came across to me and knelt in front of me.

"Are you happy for me to punish you?"

"Yes, Miss Bella."

"I've never done this before."

"I think you'll be a quick learner, Miss Bella."

"Over my lap."

Gina stood and laid herself over me, settling into a comfortable position. She was wearing a loose knee-length dress and I lifted the hem until it was sitting above her waist. Her legs and bum were exposed, as were a pair of plain white briefs. She looked gorgeous.

I took a moment to gather myself and work out what I was going to do. It hit me I wasn't nervous; I wanted to do this. I let my hand slide over her covered bum, enjoying the coolness of her skin before I warmed it. I raised my arm and brought it down for the first time. Gina reacted to the impact with only a slight movement; she was used to this. I repeated the action, letting my hand stroke her between each strike.

As I got into a rhythm, Gina relaxed and calmly took her punishment. No noise, little movement. Just the occasional short bleat, deep in her throat. I varied the point of impact and increased the force, using her thighs as well; they looked so tempting.

I stopped abruptly, as I realised that feeling had returned. The feeling I had when I watched someone being punished. But this time, I wasn't watching. I was the one inflicting the pain, and the feeling was intense, filling my being. It was a tension, but a pleasant one; enjoyment at someone else's submission. It fired me up, gave me a feeling of power. It turned me on, too. My body was filling with desire.

I came back to the present and looked at Kara. She was smiling; aware, I think, of my epiphany. I returned my gaze to Gina's bum. It was laying there, ready for me, inviting me to do anything I wanted. I made myself comfortable and yanked her knickers down her legs, pulling them off and throwing them across the room. I leaned to her ear.

"I'm going to hurt you, Gina."

"Yes, Miss Bella. I'm ready."

I lifted my arm and brought my hand down hard on her bum; she jumped, and I brought it down again before she settled. I gave her a series of regular strokes, moving it around her bum, occasionally striking her thighs. Her skin was turning pink now; a beautiful colour I was to come to love.

I stopped and rested my hand on her thigh, allowing my fingers to slip between her legs. She opened them, allowing me access. I soon saw the moisture on the inside of her thighs and followed it to her sex. She let out a sharp gasp as I let my fingers stray over her pussy and flick her clit. She was squirming at my touch.

"Legs together," I said, removing my hand.

"Yes, Miss Bella."

Before she finished speaking, I struck again, my hand now coming down on her bum rapidly and with as much force I could manage. I was almost in a trance. My body was crying out, needing this rush of adrenaline. Needing to use the woman on my lap. I'd never had a feeling like it.

Gina wasn't quiet now. Each impact produced a grunt or a groan and her legs were kicking occasionally when I managed to hit the right spot. My other arm was holding her in position firmly as I laid into her now bruised flesh.

I slid my hand between her legs, and she flung them open. The room was quiet as the impact stopped, except for Gina's heavy breathing, which increased as my fingers slid into her and fucked her roughly. Her orgasm came quickly, wracking her body, as she let out a piercing squeal. Her legs went rigid, then fell limply as she passed the peak, her upper body slumping onto the sofa.

My own breathing was heavy, my body needing what I'd given Gina. I looked over at Kara. She was watching keenly and nodded to me.

"Now take what you want," she said.

"Up, Gina," I said.

She slipped off my lap to her knees. I stood and stripped in record time before sitting back down. Surprising myself, I grabbed her hair, pulling her head between my spreading legs. She didn't need further instruction and began to eat me greedily. I pushed her head further into me until she was where I needed her and held it there.

She was an expert at this; I rose to a massive orgasm, my body jerking and trembling as it passed through me. My hands still forcing Gina's mouth onto my ravenous sex. I wanted more; I didn't want it to stop. As I recovered from the first wave, I pushed her onto her back on the floor and squatted, lowering my pussy over her mouth again, looking down her body to her open legs and wet groin.

I leaned over her and used my free hand to slap the inside of her thighs as I pressed my pussy onto her mouth. Her hands came around my legs and pulled me even closer. I thrust my fingers into her again and fucked her with them.

We came almost together, my cries filling the room. Hers muffled as I ground my sex on her mouth, but I felt her pussy spasm around my fingers.

I slid forwards, allowing Gina to breathe, and slumped onto her. I looked at Kara, who had her skirt up and was playing with herself. I rolled off the body under me.

"Gina ... Go and ..."

She was between Kara's legs in a moment and I watched as she brought her mistress to a climax. Gina was on her knees and I could see the results of my work. Her bum and thighs were red; a deep, blotchy red. I still didn't understand the thrill it gave me, but I was to learn its power and satisfaction in the coming months.

"Gina was right," Kara said with a grin. "Looks like you will be a quick learner. You enjoyed that, didn't you?"

"Yes."

"I saw the gleam in your eye."

"I've never felt anything like it."

She chuckled, as Gina slid onto the floor beside her, and Kara slowly stroked her hair.

"Power?"

"Yes.

"Lust?"

"Yes."

"A desire to hurt Gina?"

I paused before answering.

"Yes. Is that wrong?"

"No, but it needs to be controlled. That's what you need to learn."

"Did I go too far?" I asked Gina.

She looked at me with a hint of shyness.

"No, Miss Bella. I've taken more severe punishment." She looked at Kara, who smiled back. "I enjoyed it."

"You certainly seemed to, my pet. Now, let's look at the results."

Gina rose and bent over the chair, and I joined Kara to examine my handiwork. Her bum was red all over, as were her thighs.

"Pretty good," Kara said. "Nicely spread. You can play with that."

"How?"

"Sometimes you do this, a nice general covering. But you can also concentrate on one area. That gives a different result, doesn't it, Gina?"

"Yes, ma'am."

"The pain rises quicker if it's in one spot," Kara continued. "It's not necessarily as stimulating, is it?"

"No, ma'am."

"I use it more as a straight punishment. It's the same with implements; spread them around and this little thing will get as wet as a sponge. But give her several blows in one place and she knows she's being punished, rather than indulged."

She leaned down to Gina.

"Fetch some cream."

Gina got up and went over to a cupboard, bringing back a bottle of Kara's lotion. I held out my hand.

"I'd like to do it," I said.

Gina looked at Kara who nodded and she resumed her position, bent over the sofa. I took some of the lotion in my hands and began to rub it gently in. Kara reached for the bottle and joined me in soothing Gina's damaged skin. She moved sinuously as we did so, obviously enjoying the attention.

Kara winked at me and slid her fingers between Gina's legs as I continued to massage her bum. Gina began to moan and squirm, her legs opening, inviting Kara's attention. Her body slowly rose from the cushions as her orgasm approached and she grunted as it swept through her.

I felt the muscles in her bum clench and relax several times before she flopped down again, panting. Kara removed her fingers and I stopped stroking. Gina was face down in the upholstery, and her voice was muffled, but clear enough.

"Thank you, ma'am. Thank you, Miss Bella."

Chapter 18 - Madame Górska

I didn't understand my new role, but I knew I'd found my forte. Kara was kind enough to let me practice on Gina and Gina ... Well, Gina seemed more than happy to have two mistresses for a while. She positively purred when we had a training session.

Things moved quickly. Gina's friend, Mark, came to see me. He was a handsome guy in his mid-twenties, well-spoken and intelligent. He hadn't performed on camera before, but he seemed interested and asked me a stream of questions. He agreed to do it if the scenario was right when we came to shoot.

I freed up the money I needed to buy the equipment and went to see Nigel.

"Didn't think I'd see you again," he said.

"I'm full of surprises."

"Yea. I can see that." He was looking at the list of kit I wanted to order. "You're not messing about, are you?"

"No point in going off half-cocked."

He grinned and filled out the order sheet. When he'd finished, he totted it up and turned it to show me. I tried to keep a neutral expression as I saw it in black and white. It was what I expected, but it was still a huge sum of money.

"Half now," I said. "Half on delivery?"

I prayed I was doing the right thing.

I then met Steve. I'd been talking to Kara about the financial side of the venture. With my limited knowledge, it occurred to me I needed to set up a company to manage what I was doing. She'd come back a few days later to say I should meet Steve. I guessed he was a client, but it wasn't polite to ask.

He was an accountant and went through my options, offering to do the work for me. In the end, we set up a company but had to find a name.

"They're usually ridiculously corny," Kara said.

"I know. So, let's do something different."

"Don't look at me, it's your company."

"I've been thinking about that."

"About what?"

"Want to run it with me?"

"I don't know anything about running a business."

"Nor do I, so I fancy having someone to bounce things off."

"What about Marco?"

"I offered."

"And?"

"I offered him a percentage of the company in exchange for his distribution contacts."

"What did he say?"

"No."

"So, you've lost the distribution side."

"I didn't say that."

"Come on," she said, "tell me."

"He thinks I'll fail. He didn't want a piece of the action because he doesn't think there will be any. He wants a one-off payment."

"How much?"

"Ten thousand."

"What! Is it worth it?"

"I don't know, but I've agreed."

"Bella, if it's not too rude, where is all this money coming from?"

I told her briefly about my father and his legacy, without naming names. Then about the money I'd saved.

"There's more to you than first appears, isn't there?" she said when I finished.

"Do you want in?"

"How do you mean?"

"Co-owner."

"What?"

"Look, I need you to help me with this. I need your experience and guidance and I'll admit I wouldn't mind using this place as a set sometimes." She gave a gentle nod at that suggestion. "I can pay you by the hour if you like, but how about you take a stake in the company?"

"What would it cost me?"

"Nothing; well a few quid, I think. The money I've put in will be a loan and will have first call on profits until it's repaid. But above that, you'll share the profits."

"But I'm not investing anything."

"You are. Without you – and Gina – I wouldn't have been able to start this."

We talked around in circles; Kara could see the logic to my argument but was unsure about getting involved. Eventually, she spoke to Steve who convinced her to accept. There was little risk and if we were successful, she would benefit. She took twenty-five per cent of the shares in Karabella Productions Limited.

Marco was stunned when I paid him the ten thousand but was good as his word. Over the next month, he introduced me to three men who were to be crucial in the success or failure of our little venture. One had a chain of shops in Britain, another had a wholesale and mail order business in Germany, and the other was a distributor across Europe.

I met with each of them and explained what I was going to do. They were all interested and agreed to take the first three films we produced to see if there was any demand.

Marco also agreed I could borrow Andy – when he didn't need him – and approach a couple of his girls to see if they would work with me.

"Just make sure they're unmarked when I need them," he said.

Andy was amazed when he saw the kit stacked in my spare bedroom. We spent the afternoon unpacking it, inspecting it, putting it together. He was like a kid in a sweetshop.

"I haven't used most of this," he said. "But it shouldn't take too long. The principles the same. Can I take a camera to try it out?"

"Yea. Just remember where you found it and keep it away from Marco."

He grinned.

"Not a word."

He spent a couple of days wandering around filming with the high definition camera, then a day trying some editing. The results were staggering, so much better than we were used to.

"Nigel's right," he said. "This is the future."

"What's all the stuttering on the picture?"

"I think it's this place," he said. "This film's more sensitive than the old tape I'm used to. We're going to have to find somewhere rock solid and sound-proofed."

An unexpected source helped with that. I always rang Kara before I visited, I didn't want to interrupt anything. When I called her the next day, she hesitated before inviting me over and as I approached the turning into her mews, I spotted a large black Mercedes parked in the street. I immediately recognised the driver and knew who Kara's guest must be.

The driver jumped when I rapped on the window, turning sharply to look at me, before relaxing and breaking into a broad grin. He opened the door, got out and gave me a big hug.

"Bella, it's great to see you. How are you doing?"

"Hi, Dave. Good to see you. I'm about to meet your boss."

He looked puzzled for a moment. "I'm visiting Kara."

"You know her?"

"Yea. Business associates."

He grinned.

"You're doing okay, then."

"I hope so."

I gave him a peck on the cheek and went to Kara's.

"Come in," she said. "I've got a guest."

"Yea, I know," I replied. "Morning, Sonny," I called out before we'd left the hallway. Kara gave me a questioning look.

"Good morning, Annabelle," he replied as we entered the main room.

"How did you know?" Kara asked.

"Annabelle knows my driver," Sonny said, remembering the connection. "They worked together."

"We did," I replied. "We've just had a cuddle."

"Don't expect it excited him."

"Probably not."

"You two seem to have hit it off. I gather you're going into business together."

"Yup."

"Need anything?"

"Funny you should say that."

Sonny came up trumps. He offered us an underground warren of rooms.

"Had it for years," he said when he showed us around. "It was built during the war, but nobody wants it now. It'll need doing up a bit, but there's power and water and it's completely hidden and secure."

It sure was; about twenty feet underground with solid concrete walls and a discreet entrance behind an anonymous door between two shops.

When Andy saw it, he was delighted.

"It's just right. No outside noises or vibrations."

"It's got other uses, as well."

I showed him around the various rooms.

"These would make great sets," he said.

"Exactly; all sorts of possibilities."

"What are you going to call yourself?" Gina asked.

"What do you mean?" I said. She looked bashful for a moment.

"Well ... I thought you might ... use a different name."

It hadn't crossed my mind.

"She's right, you know," Kara said. "Bella isn't right for a ferocious Domme."

As I thought about what they said, I knew they were right. Bella was a soft name; fine for someone taking punishment, but not for someone controlling the scene.

"I don't know," I said. "Any suggestions?"

They threw names about; other dominatrices they knew and a few concocted mouthfuls.

"Some of those are embarrassing," I said.

"I know," Kara replied, laughing.

"What does it need?" I asked.

"Needs to sound strong ..."

"With a hint of sex ...

"What's your middle name?" Gina asked.

I frowned at her until she looked away.

"Come on," Kara said. "Tell us."

"I'm Annabelle Helena Charlotte Giselle."

They looked at one another, trying not to laugh.

"Go on," I said. "Make something out of that."

We played with them all, but Charlotte and Giselle were like Annabelle; too soft.

"Helena, Helen," Kara mused. "It's not too bad."

"I could make something up," I said.

"True, but it's better to have a connection with it. It's more personal."

"Helena hurts," Gina said.

"Well, that's the idea," I said.

"No," she replied, allowing her frustration to show for a second or two. "Helena Hertz; H..E..R..T..Z."

"Sounds good," Kara said. "What about Helena von Hertz?"

"But then you don't get the pun on the phrase," Gina said. She clearly liked her idea and was willing to push for it. It worked. I had found my professional name; a name which became increasingly interchangeable with my own.

"The only thing you need now are some clothes," Kara said.

"I've got plenty of underwear."

"No, Bella. You need something special; you need to stand out. You're one of the few women I have to look up to, literally. Use that height to the full and it adds to your mystique. You haven't seen my work wardrobe, have you?"

"No."

"Come with us."

They took me into the room at the back of the house; it was a mass of rails, drawers, and boxes. As Kara showed me what she wore for work, I saw what she meant. I had nothing like this. Corsets, boots, basques; made from a variety of materials. Some were gorgeous and I imagined Kara wearing them; I could see why she impressed her clients.

"You could borrow these if we were the same size, but none of this will fit you."

She was much more muscular than me, but I was a few inches taller.

"No," she said. "You need to see Madame Górska."

Madame Górska lived and worked in a flower-covered terraced house in Ealing. The ground floor had once been a shop and she used it as her workplace. My first impression of that space was one of utter bedlam, material everywhere. Garments in various stages of completion resting on every surface, some looking as if they'd been untouched for years. I was to learn everything was exactly where Madame Górska wanted it, and woe betide anyone who moved it.

The woman herself was sitting at an ancient treadle sewing machine, intently stitching some deep red material. She didn't look up as we entered; Kara waited patiently, not saying a word. After scanning the room, I turned my attention to the woman we'd come to see. She was probably around sixty, though it was difficult to tell. She had a look of maternal warmth, but there was an air of melancholy about her.

Finally, she lifted the machine foot, and pulled the material away, cutting the threads. She took off the glasses she'd been wearing and slipped on another pair that had been resting on her head. Looking up, she squinted at us.

"Ah, Kara, my dear. How nice to see you."

She rose and came over to Kara and gave her a hug.

"And who is this?" she asked.

"This," Kara replied, "is Bella, a friend of mine."

"Well," Madame said. "Welcome, Bella."

"Hello, Madame Górska," I replied. It was oddly formal.

"Bella needs something special. Something to make her look like a real mistress."

I was slightly taken aback. The woman in front of me didn't look like someone familiar with the world of dominatrices and fetish. How wrong I was.

"I see," she said. "Anything in mind?"

"No," Kara replied. "I thought you could use your judgement."

"Walk around," she said to me. "Let me see how you move."

I did as I was told, trying to place her accent. Her English was almost perfect, but there was the odd stress or tone I couldn't place. Occasionally a touch of French, but then something which sounded East European.

"How long?" Madame asked.

"Ideally, about a week," Kara replied.

"Always in a rush, you girls. Always in a rush. Strip Bella."

I was momentarily disconcerted but quickly stripped to my underwear. Madame proceeded to measure almost every bit of me, carefully noting all the figures on a scrap of paper. She stepped back and took one final look at me.

"Ready Monday," she said and went over to her sewing machine and returned to her work. I quickly dressed and followed Kara out of the door.

"That's it?" I asked.

"Yes, that's it."

"What am I getting?"

"Who knows? Only Madame Górska. But you won't be disappointed."

"Who is she?"

"If you believe the stories, she comes from a Polish family who escaped during the war. But she's never spoken to me about it, so I'm not sure."

"How did you find her?"

"Oh, she's well known to lots of people in the industry. She provides stuff for lots of the girls I know."

"You wouldn't think so, looking at her."

"No. But she's nowhere near as innocent as she looks."

We returned the following Monday, to find Madame in exactly the same position; hunched over her sewing machine. She acknowledged us when she was ready.

"Ah," she said. "There you are."

She swapped glasses again, and went over to an unusually clear counter, picking up a black garment.

"Strip off," she said to me; I obeyed. She had a manner which was kindly but brooked little argument.

When I was down to my knickers, she opened the garment up; I could see it was a corset. She held it to the floor, I stepped into it and she carefully lifted it, until it was in the right place. I adjusted my breasts and she went around the back to tighten the lacing.

I looked at the part I could see. It was black with a satin sheen, almost certainly silk, but with a layer of padding around the bones. Thin red lines ran vertically every half an inch. It looked fabulous. I flinched as she gave a few final tugs to the lacing.

"Take a look," she said.

I went over to the full-length mirror on the wall and smiled as soon as I looked into it. It fitted perfectly, accentuating my shape in all the right places, and giving me a beautiful cleavage.

"I thought these ..." Madame said, handing me a pair of long black gloves. I carefully put them on, they came nearly to the shoulder.

"Well?" Kara asked.

"It's fabulous," I replied. "I feel ... well, it's wonderful." I turned to Madame. "Thank you."

She gave a little shrug.

"It was all I could do in the time. Give me more notice next time, young lady."

I returned to the mirror and twisted so I could see it from the sides. I had to admit, it made me look good and the gloves were a great addition.

"You look good, girl," Kara said. I'd noticed her watching me.

"These are the suspenders," Madame said. "Which attach here." She pointed to tiny reinforced spots along the hem. "And I made a halter, but you don't need to use it."

She put the extras in a little bag and tied it. As she loosened the lacing, I pulled the gloves off and she put everything into a bag as I got dressed again.

"How much do I owe you?" I asked.

"I haven't worked it out yet."

"But I must pay you."

She seemed unconcerned.

"I'll put it on your account, all the girls have one. Some aren't always able to pay, and I give them time."

"Oh, okay. But please let me know."

"Pay me the next time. You'll be back."

Chapter 19 - Film Star

"Everyone ready?" Andy asked.

We were starting our first shoot. I was dressed in Madame Górska's corset and gloves, with black stockings, calf-length red patent leather boots, and tight red briefs. I'd loosed my hair at Kara's suggestion and it hung over my shoulders and back. Gina had done my make-up; more than I was used to, but it somehow looked right.

Cassie was naked and tied to one of the rings in the wall of Kara's stable room. Her feet were just touching the floor. Andy had finally stopped fiddling with the lighting and was ready with the camera. We hadn't been able to get another cameraman, so we'd have to do lots of re-shoots and angle changes.

Kara had placed a chair in the corner to watch and make suggestions and Gina had somehow made herself indispensable and was sitting at Kara's feet. Cassie and I had agreed the outline of what we were going to do with input from both of them. Andy and I were jointly directing everything, which we knew could be a recipe for disaster, but I wasn't sure how far he could free himself from Marco's formulaic methods.

For the first hour or so, I took it slowly; I knew I was going to take time to relax and settle in. A lot of what we shot ended up being discarded, but as I got into the mood, my confidence grew, and I began to enjoy myself. I felt that thrill, even though we kept on stopping to move things around.

We improvised dialogue, although I did most of the talking as Cassie was supposed to be the unwilling victim. I used a crop to lightly mark her; her breasts, her thighs and tummy. She was a good recipient; she knew how to act the part, even though I soon saw she was enjoying it. My gloves looked good against her skin and when I used them between her legs, the colour contrast looked good on screen.

When I turned her to face the wall, I switched to the flogger and set to work on her back. I found myself talking far more than I had planned, but Andy and Kara both thought it worked, so I carried on. By the time Cassie's back and thighs were nicely marked, I could tell she was worked up and forced my hand between her legs, fingering her to a vocal orgasm.

We took a break for lunch.

"Okay?" I asked Cassie.

"Yea. That was good. I liked the stuff you were saying. I know I'm supposed to be frightened and I hope I looked scared, but it worked for me."

"Yes," Kara said. "We noticed."

"Can't help it," Cassie replied. "I've come to like this stuff."

After lunch, I tied her slowly over a table and gave her a caning before teasing her with my fingers and a dildo. I was testing myself as well. I tried to delay her orgasm as long as possible; taking her close and stopping until she was wailing in frustration.

There was one thing I had forgotten; how much doing this would turn me on. I was frustrated too. We'd decided there wouldn't be any sex other than me using my fingers or toys to make Cassie come. I hadn't taken my own needs into account.

Eventually, with some demanding dialogue from me, I brought Cassie to orgasm. It was intense, her body shaking and convulsing. Her cries and obscenities echoed around the room. When she recovered, I tied her to the wall ring again and walked out through the door. Apart from Cassie acting some face shots to go with her orgasm, filming was done for the day.

"Well?" I asked Kara and Gina, when Andy and Cassie had left. They looked at each other.

"I think that worked," Kara said, and gave me a wry smile. "Did it work for you?"

"Yes," I replied. "I forgot about that bit."

"Need some help?"

"Wouldn't say no."

The next day, it was Mark's turn. The scenario was similar, except we started with him in briefs; I didn't want to reveal his assets too quickly. Again, I used the crop and the flogger on him. He had a muscular body and the reactions of those muscles to the implements were captured by the camera. It looked stunning.

After lunch, I gave him a caning and finally got him to lie on his back, his cock now clearly visible and stiff. It was beautiful. I'd seen so many cocks in my life and they were all different. Short, long, thin, fat. All sorts of angles, colours, and shapes. But some were just beautiful, and Mark's was one of them.

I slowly wrapped some rubber tubing around his cock and balls, keeping it tight. His cock swelled, the veins standing proud and purple and I slowly went to work with my fingers, teasing him as I had Cassie. I'd never spent any time doing this, but I knew it was a popular fetish. It seemed to come naturally, and I loved it, listening to his moans of frustration as I stopped short of his climax.

I would have loved to have jumped on and ridden it, I needed it. But I kept going, taunting him with more improvised dialogue. Eventually, he let me know it was getting too painful. I got him to beg for release and I gently rubbed his frenulum with my thumb.

When he came, it was spectacular. His cum shot high in the air, his hips jumping off the floor. He kept coming, his cock jerking seven or eight times, expelling a full load each time. He was grunting loudly with each spasm. I wondered when it would end, but eventually, he relaxed, his chest heaving.

My gloves were covered in his cum, and when Andy stopped filming, I burst out laughing. Mark looked at me with embarrassment on his face.

"Sorry," he said.

"Don't be," I replied. "That'll look great on film. You're a heavy cummer."

"I am when I'm really turned on."

"Did that work, then?"

He looked slightly embarrassed again.

"Yes," he whispered.

When we were alone, Kara offered Gina's services again, but I refused.

"I can't keep on imposing myself," I said. "I need to find someone."

Kara understood, but Gina looked a little disappointed. That evening I went out, and for the first time in ages, picked up a random guy at a bar.

"Was he any good?" Kara asked when I told her.

"Eventually."

"Eventually?"

"He wasn't expecting to be used quite so much."

"He was expecting a wham, bam, thank you, ma'am?"

"Yup. But he got himself a demanding bitch instead."

"Did he make the grade?"

"Yea, once he relaxed and let me run things."

"Going to give him another go?"

"I doubt it. He'd run a mile if he ever saw me again."

A week later, we were ready to film the final scene for our first release. This time we were in the concrete warren using a new set we'd dressed, and we had both Mark and Cassie. We'd had to wait for them to heal. We were planning a scene with both of them and we spent some time talking through how it would work.

Eventually, we did something similar to the first two scenes, but with both of them. I teased and punished them both individually, then made Mark get on his hands and knees. Cassie was made to lie on top of him, assuming the same shape. With him supporting her body, I caned her, her reactions being transmitted to his body underneath. It looked good on film.

When they swapped, I couldn't do the same. He was rock solid now, and his cock would have been pressing into Cassie. I did notice her looking at his erection several times with an interested expression, but we had consciously decided not to feature sex in our films.

So, I placed her on all fours, with his body resting on her at right angles. It gave an interesting angle for the camera. In one shot, you saw me caning him, with her bruised bum to one side.

When I finished the punishment, I made them tease each other. Mark using his fingers to edge Cassie, finally allowing him to take her to orgasm when she begged me. Her need was real enough.

Then Cassie edged Mark; she was good. She was clearly enjoying playing with his cock and I had to reprimand her a couple of times. Eventually, I let him come and he repeated his earlier performance, his cum shooting high in the air and much of it landing on Cassie. This time, it was her turn to suppress her surprise.

I'd made a change to this shoot. I was going to take some pleasure. When they'd recovered and cleaned up, I made them use their fingers and a dildo on me. I knew what my new role did to me, and it didn't take them long to give me two intense orgasms. We finished with me spent in a chair, and Cassie and Mark on the floor either side of me.

After Cassie and Mark left, I changed and arranged to meet Andy the next day to start editing. I left the technical side to him, but we shared the decision-making and after two days, we had something we were pleased with. After some over-dubs, and the addition of music, we looked at each other.

"That's a winner," he said.

"Let's not be too optimistic."

"Oh, come on, Bella. They're three great scenes in high definition; it'll go down a storm."

It did. We knew the number of homes with DVD players was still small compared with VHS, but we ordered similar numbers, hoping we'd sell them. I had a few copies couriered to my distributors. They all rang me to say the films looked great and they sold them on the first day. In a month, we sold over a thousand copies; nearly half were DVDs. It was definitely the way forward.

We'd set up an e-mail address and began to receive feedback from customers. Most of it was very favourable; some of it was creepy. We expected that. Gina took on the role of admin, and we tried to respond to everyone who contacted us. When we were in the office, she'd often read us the latest mails. Many of them were unintentionally hilarious, some made us retch, and a few were sad. But they also gave us ideas and challenges. One of the most frequent requests was one we'd anticipated, and we were to find an unexpected way of satisfying it.

We produced one film a month for the first few months, and every one flew off the shelves. I got a huge amount of fan mail and a lot of interesting offers. The buyers loved what we were doing, both the content and the quality. But there was a recurring demand for sex in some of the scenes.

I had found another guy willing to act with us, Sean. He wasn't as good as Mark, but he had a distinctive look and was heavily tattooed; he gave us entry into another niche market. Word had got around, and two of the girls who worked for Mark had come to ask if we could use them. Cassie and Mark were still the core; they worked well with me, and together.

I asked everyone involved with us to come to a meeting one day.

"I wanted to have a chat about where we are and where we're going," I said. I told them how many films we'd sold. In six months, it amounted to more than ten thousand copies. Andy had already told me Marco didn't sell that many in a year, and he'd been going a long time. Apparently, he was desperate to know how we were doing, but Andy hadn't told him.

I thanked everyone and gave them each a bonus, determined by how many scenes they'd done for me. I was generous by nature, but it would help keep them on side. The reactions told me I'd got that right.

Before I wrapped up, I mentioned the sex element.

"I know initially we weren't going to include full sex scenes, and I still want to continue making the films we're doing without them. But if any of you know people who would be good at this and be happy to add sex, please point them in my direction. I'm not forcing anyone to do things they don't want to do."

After the meeting, a couple of the girls asked if sex would pay extra; I told them it would. They went off to think about it. Mark and Cassie came back into the office where Gina and I were clearing up. Kara was watching us; she had assumed a non-working role in the enterprise, but her input was still priceless. She had a knack for knowing what worked and what didn't.

"Bella?" Cassie said.

"Yes, Cas?"

"Mark and I are happy to shoot sex scenes."

"Okay."

"But only with each other."

She gave him a look that told me why.

"Oh, yes."

"Well ..." she said, "we're sort of ..."

Kara burst out laughing and Mark blushed.

"Couldn't resist that beautiful cock, eh, Cassie?" I said.

"No," she replied. "Yes ... there's more to it than that."

"I'm only joking. We'll have a chat about what you're prepared to do. You're our most popular actors anyway, so the two of you together will be dynamite."

"We might be prepared to work with you, as well," she said.
"Oh?"

She looked nervous for the first time; she was clearly the spokesperson for the couple.

"But we'd want Mark to cover up."

I'd guessed that was the issue and I could understand it. The porn industry in the States had been ravaged by HIV and Aids, and condoms were increasingly common in mainstream porn.

"I think that would be an excellent idea," I said. "We'll see." I turned away, before slowly going back to them. "I wouldn't mind trying that beautiful cock."

Chapter 20 - Alice

The next year was a time of increasing success and popularity. We were making a couple of films a month and all sold well. Even Kara joined in, making a few films. She had control of her style and we released them as a separate series. She only worked with girls and the films were softer, more sensual, but they found a ready market. A lot of her correspondence came from female customers.

I got a call from Marco and he came to see me. He was gobsmacked when I showed him around. We now had four permanent sets, and a couple of spaces we dressed as needed. We'd found two good part-time cameramen and one editing room had grown to two. Andy had found a young woman straight out of film school, Becky, who was unfazed by the material she was working with and full of ideas. They worked together to tighten up our editing and improve the look and sound of our films, giving them a house style.

Gina had been overwhelmed by the admin side and we employed a friend of hers, Alice, who joined us full-time. She was so efficient, Gina had been able to pull back a little.

When I brought Marco to the office, Alice and Gina were answering e-mails and Kara was being Kara, sitting in a comfortable chair, drinking coffee and supervising. He took some coffee and dropped into another chair, shaking his head.

"I don't believe it," he said. "I really don't."

"No faith, Marco."

"This is like a professional set-up."

"No, Marco. It *is* a professional set-up; I don't mess about." I paused and took a few sips of coffee. "How's business?" Kara gave me a silent grin.

"Not so good," Marco replied. "I'm thinking of packing it in. You've taken most of my team."

"They're free to work for you whenever they want."

"I know, I'm not complaining. I guess I didn't keep up."

"Something like that."

"I don't fancy changing all my equipment and learning everything again. Can't afford it, to be honest."

"It's not cheap, I'll admit, but it was worth it."

"Yea, I've seen some of your films. They're good and the quality is amazing."

"I'll buy you out," I said.

He looked at me as if I'd hit him.

"What?"

"I'll buy you out. All your kit, all your back catalogue and your brand names; everything."

He looked at each of us, stunned. Eventually, he slumped in his chair.

"I was hoping I might be able to work for you," he said wearily.

"Sorry, Marco. You said it yourself; you don't fancy learning everything again. I can't work with someone with that attitude."

I knew it was harsh, but it was true. I knew it, and he knew it. After a couple of weeks, we made the deal. I bought everything and incorporated it into our company. He promised not to produce similar films for five years and he kept his promise. The last I heard, he was running a pub in Essex.

The deal led to us expanding and going into the male domination market. Troy came over to us and I let him run with that side. I knew he was good, and he knew people I didn't. He soon found several new actors, and we found ourselves releasing a new film every ten days or so, under four different series titles.

One evening after everyone had left, I was closing up and was surprised to find Alice still in the office.

"I thought you'd gone," I said.

"No, just finishing off."

Alice had proved herself something of an office wizard. She coped with anything we threw at her and had ideas of her own. She had also given me a few pleasant dreams. She was a few years younger than me; shorter and a little stockier, but with long blonde hair and an impish smile. I'd imagined doing a few things with her.

"Happy working here?" I asked. I hadn't sat down with her since she'd started.

"Loving it, thank you. You leave me to get on with it and everyone's so friendly and supportive."

"Yea. Worked anywhere like this before?"

"In offices, yes. But not doing what you do here."

"Were you shocked?"

"Not really. Gina had told me what you did."

"How did you know Gina?"

She paused, and I realised the question was too personal.

"Sorry," I said. "Forget that, I didn't mean to pry."

"It's okay. We met at a BDSM group."

"Oh." That was interesting. "So, you're into all this?"

She hesitated.

"Yes ... No ... I mean ... I think so."

"Ah, exploring."

"Yes. When Gina talked about you and what you were doing ..."

"You wanted to find out."

"Yes. Sorry."

"Don't apologise. You're ideal for us. But are you getting what you wanted?"

She gave me the most gorgeous smile.

"Not yet," she said. "But I'm hoping I will."

It was an obvious come on.

"Looking for a personal connection or a professional one?" I asked.

"Oh, personal; I think."

"Doing anything tonight?"

"No, Miss Bella."

"You have been talking to Gina," I said with a laugh. "We'd better see if you can be as good as she is."

"I hope so, ma'am."

I went to take her home but paused. Everything we needed was right here.

"Come here, Alice," I said.

She got up from her desk and came to stand in front of me.

"Sure you want to do this?" I asked her.

"Yes. If I don't try, I'll never know, will I?"

"Want to start right now?"

Her eyes widened as she thought for a few seconds. Her face slowly softened and took on a look of expectancy.

"Yes, ma'am."

I walked slowly around her; she stood still. I took in her shape, her skin, her hair.

"I'd like to see what I'm dealing with, Alice."

Unbidden, she unzipped her skirt, dropping it to the floor, revealing a nice pair of black stockings. She unbuttoned her blouse and removed it. Underneath, a lacy black bra with a matching suspender belt and black thong. She looked tempting as hell. The bra came off and I looked at her breasts, her nipples already telling me this was what she wanted.

"That's enough for now," I said. Standing closely in front of her, I let my fingers trail over her breasts, and she closed her eyes, a long sigh escaping her lips. She jumped and her eyes opened wide as I gave her a light kiss on those lips. A little bleat sent a shiver through me. I pulled an inch away from her mouth.

"On your knees."

She dropped to her haunches, looking up at me. Her expression told me she was mine. At that moment, she'd do

151

anything. I had to remember this was new for her, I needed to be careful.

"Follow me."

As I walked, she followed, crawling on her hands and knees. I led her to the smallest set we had, with a couple of hanging bars, a horse, and a couch.

"Stand."

She got to her feet, her hands behind her back.

"You've thought about this?"

"Yes, ma'am, and dreamed about it."

"What did you dream of?"

"Obeying you, ma'am. Being punished if I didn't."

"Is that what you want?"

Her breathing was erratic for a few seconds, her eyes flashing with need.

"Yes, ma'am."

"You will stop me if you need to, Alice."

"Yes, ma'am."

"Good girl."

This elicited a sharp groan. I led her to the bar.

"Hands up."

She grabbed the bar with both hands.

"I'm not going to tie you, not the first time. But I want you to hold on."

She nodded vigorously. I stood behind her, my mouth close to her ear.

"I'm going to enjoy this, Alice. I'm going to hurt you; spank this gorgeous ass of yours." I ran my hand lightly over her bum and her body quivered at my touch. "Let's see if you can take it."

Before she had a chance to reply, I brought my hand down hard on her skin; she let out a little cry. After a few strokes, she pushed her hips back to meet my hand.

"Too soft, am I?" I said and increased the force. She was letting out little moans on each stroke. I stopped and pushed my fingers between her legs; her thong was wet.

"We can do without this."

I pulled the thong down and she stepped out of it.

"I think you need more than a spanking, Alice."

I picked up a flogger from the table and her eyes followed me as I walked in front of her, letting it slide through my hands. I moved behind her, and stopped, letting her anticipation grow. When her body finally relaxed, I gently flicked the flogger over her back. The first stroke prompted a gasp, but she recovered and her body hardly flinched.

Moving to her front, I let it gently play over her breasts. She let her head fall back and pushed them forward, a squeal coming as one of the fronds caught her nipple. Her tummy received the same treatment, and she took it all, even when I let the flogger stray between her legs.

When I stopped, she focussed on me. Her eyes had a distant look; I knew that look. She was already lost in the moment. I was surprised.

"Is this really your first time, Alice?"

"Yes, ma'am. Except in my dreams, so many dreams."

"I've had a few dreams about you too, Alice. Over the horse."

She let go of the bar and walked over to the horse, bending over it, and stretching her arms so her hands could grasp the end. Her bum was so inviting. I knelt by her head.

"I'm going to flog your ass, Alice. I'm going to flog it hard and I'm going to enjoy it."

"Yes, ma'am."

"You will tell me if it gets too much, Alice."

"Yes, ma'am."

I got into position. I did this regularly on camera. I was good at it and loved it, and it showed in our films. But apart from Gina, this was the first time I'd had the chance to do this in a private situation, to someone who was asking me to do it. The thrill was there and building, but it was different; the feeling was stronger, deeper. I understood how Kara must feel with Gina. This was fun, not work.

And it needed a slight change. I put the flogger down and stripped. I only had casual clothes on, so took them all off.

Picking up the flogger again, I walked around the horse, until I was in front of Alice. The look on her face as she let her eyes take in my nakedness was one of pure desire; I felt the same way.

"If you're a good girl," I said, "there will be some pleasure."

She gave an imploring smile, and I felt a growing warmth in my groin; it spurred me on. I returned to the other end of the horse and took position. Raising my arm, I brought the fronds down hard on her bum. She gave a sharp moan before the flogger bit again, and again.

My lust was up, and I used it hard and fast on her skin. Hitting her bum and thighs as her body writhed under the onslaught. I was in a trance, letting that lust out on Alice. Her cries and moans were almost constant, fuelling an overwhelming feeling of desire.

Breaking my rhythm, I thrust a hand between her legs and her body jumped into the air. I drove three fingers into her pussy, and she spread her legs. She was dripping wet and as I fucked her with my hand, her orgasm came quickly, rippling through her body. Her cries filled the small room and I was jealous of her pleasure.

As she came down, still clearly needing more, I pulled her back off the horse, winding her hair around my hand.

"Fucked women before, Alice?"

"Yes, ma'am," she panted.

"Good."

I almost dragged her to the couch, pushing her back onto it, before climbing on and straddling her face. She wrapped her arms around my thighs and gripped me as I lowered my pussy onto her mouth. I let out a long moan as her lips and tongue greedily attacked my sensitive flesh.

I stayed upright as I used her to reach my first climax, rubbing myself on her face as it hit me hard. I had to support myself as it rushed through me, my head hanging down, letting my hair flow over her open legs. I let myself come down, knowing we weren't finished yet and as feeling

154

returned to my pussy and clit, I swept my hair away and lowered myself over her groin.

With both of us past the need of our first orgasm, the urgency was gone, and we set about enjoying one another. I don't know how long we were there, but by the time I slid off Alice, we were both exhausted. I pulled her to me and kissed her. She returned it more fiercely than I expected, before pulling away, embarrassed.

"Sorry, ma'am."

"Don't be. It's not forbidden to be soft and gentle, you know."

"I'm not sure what the rules are."

"There are no rules. Every relationship is different. If it feels right for both of us, it is right."

Alice came home with me that night. We soothed her marked skin and enjoyed each other again. And we talked most of the night. About what she wanted and what I wanted. They matched closely and so began a relationship that lasted for two years, although in that time it changed beyond all recognition and went in directions I could never have imagined.

"Found someone at last," Kara said when I told her. "Good. It's about time you did this for fun rather than profit."

We were open with the whole team. Alice got some gentle ribbing from just about everyone, but it was light-hearted, and she took it in her stride. We didn't display our relationship at work. Gina and Alice still ran the office and were in charge there. They didn't defer to Kara or me until we got home.

Chapter 21 - Life Changes

Over the next year, we found a new star. It was Alice. Once she had taken the leap, she voraciously sought new experiences. It turned out she liked them all. My relationship with her was never like the one Kara had with Gina. Alice could be submissive and loved to be. She wanted to be topped by a man; I indulged her. But we soon found out she was a switch. She loved to top women; then she tried topping guys.

She loved it all and she was good. Eventually, she suggested trying it on camera. I talked to Kara, unsure of the situation.

"If she wants to," Kara said, "let her try. If she's bad, that'll be the end of it. But if she's good, we might have a new attraction."

I was disappointed. I thought I'd found a partner, a personal partner. If she joined the business, it would be different. But I wasn't going to stop her, it was her choice.

We let her shoot three scenes. In one, she topped a girl, in another she submitted to a guy and in the third, she joined me in topping Mark. We were including sex in most of our films now; not in every scene, but at least one.

When we watched the edited film, we all knew Alice was a winner. When it was released, it was one of our most successful films and we decided she should star in her own series. We called her Alicia Switch; it was corny, but it didn't matter. She became as popular as Kara and me, and that made me take stock.

I'd never set out to be a porn star, it had just happened. I didn't care if Alice or Troy or anyone else became more popular than me. I took Kara out for lunch one day.

"What's on your mind?" Kara asked when we'd ordered.

"How long do you want to do this?" I asked.

"I don't know. How long before we get told we're past it?"

"Exactly. I don't want to get to that point."

"Jealous of Alice?"

"No, but she has made me realise I'm no spring chicken anymore. I want to get out at some point."

"When?"

"I don't know."

"You don't enjoy it anymore?"

"I get a kick out of it, but ..."

"You're getting bored."

"Something like that. How about you?"

"I'm happier than I've been for years. Thanks to you, I've almost given up the dominatrix gig ..."

"Really?"

"Yup, I've got three long-termers left and I'm not taking anyone else on. I still do it on film, but that's easy and I'm not doing much of that now, either."

It was true. Kara was only doing the occasional scene, and I wasn't doing much more. The company was making significant profits and we were able to step back, letting others take the starring roles.

We were known as successful and fair players in an industry where ethics were hard to find. We had no problem finding people to act in our films. We had far more applicants than we needed and could afford to be choosy. We stood by our regulars and paid them well.

Kara and I were more businesswomen than performers now. It was fine, but I didn't want to do it forever. In the end, the decision was taken out of our hands.

"Sonny's dead."

I couldn't believe what Kara was saying.

"What? How?"

"An accident, supposedly."

"What happened?"

"Apparently he was knocked over in a hit and run. The car was found burnt out in Tottenham."

"A planned hit?"

"Sounds like it. We'll need to watch out."

It wasn't long before we felt the impact. A few weeks later we got a visit from three men. One almost as elegant as Sonny had been, the other two were heavies.

"I'm Janos," the elegant one said. "I've taken over most of Mr Luckett's ... interests."

"Oh, yes."

"I gather you rent this place from us."

I thought quickly. We'd never signed anything, and Sonny had never asked for any payment.

"Not exactly," I replied.

"Not exactly?"

"No."

"But Mr Luckett rented you these premises?"

"No."

He looked confused for a moment, before reforming his face into its usual featureless mask.

"What are you doing here, then?" he asked.

"He lent it to us."

"Lent it?"

"Yes."

"For nothing?"

"Yes."

He shook his head in mock sadness.

"Sonny, Sonny. You always were too soft. Well, ladies, I'm afraid that's about to change. We're going to want some rent."

"How much?"

"I've heard you're quite successful. Perhaps we could settle for a piece of the action."

"How much?"

"Twenty per cent."

"Of what?"

"Gross profit."

I wasn't about to give this moron twenty per cent of anything, but I knew we'd have to tread carefully.

"Can we think about it?" Kara asked.

"Sure."

"How long?"

"I'll be back this time next week."

When he left, Kara and I went for a walk.

"We're not paying it, are we?" she said.

"No way."

"What do we do?"

"I've got an idea."

As we strolled around the local park, I outlined my plan. It depended on a bit of luck, some hard work and something my European distributor had said a few weeks earlier.

A week later, Kara and I waited for Janos to appear. We'd asked Andy and Troy to be present. We weren't expecting trouble but wanted to look as if it wouldn't be a good idea to start anything. In truth, Andy and Troy were pussycats, but they were both large, well-built guys, so at least projected the right image.

When Janos came into the office, he couldn't contain his surprise. The entire complex had been gutted. We'd moved everything out. Apart from the paint on the walls and the new electrics and plumbing, the place looked like it had when Sonny had shown us around.

He studied us for a moment, then looked at Andy and Troy. His heavies had sloped off into a corner, clearly as confused as their boss. If they were the usual type for the job, they were easily confused, anyway.

"What's going on?" Janos asked.

"We're returning the keys," I said, indicating the pile on the one remaining table. Most of them didn't seem to fit anything, anyway. He flicked the pile apart with his hand.

"You can't walk away like this," he said.

"I think we can. We had no formal agreement with Sonny, no lease. Just a gentleman's agreement." He narrowed his eyes as I laid heavy stress on 'gentleman'. "As he's no longer the owner, that agreement has come to an end. So, we're returning the premises as we found them. Well, in a better state than we found them, but you can have the paint for nothing."

I was enjoying his discomfort but knew I had to be careful. He studied me for a minute or two; I held his gaze, but it got harder and harder.

"You've moved everything?"

"It would appear so."

"Don't get smart with me."

"I answered your question. If that's smart, I can't help it."

I heard a stifled laugh behind me and knew I had to bring this to an end.

"Look, Janos," I said. "Things change. Sonny let us have this place and he's gone. You're taking over and are no doubt a busy man. Take the keys and we'll leave you in peace. You'll be free to find another tenant."

"Who'd want this place?"

"Sonny had the same problem, I believe; that's why he let us use it."

He looked silently around for a while.

"Alright, get out."

We said nothing as we left the concrete warren for the last time.

"I need a drink," Andy said when we got outside. We walked a couple of streets before heading into the first pub we came across. We were all more shaken than we realised.

"The end of an era," Kara said, raising her glass. We all had mixed feelings, as it certainly was.

We hadn't told Stefan the whole story. We hadn't just moved everything; Kara and I had sold up. One of our distributors based in Germany had got involved in production, and he'd jokingly said to me at our last meeting to let him know if we ever wanted to sell the company.

I rang him and he hadn't been joking. I was honest as to why we were selling, but he hadn't been worried. He was far enough away not to be worried about Janos. As I'd done with Marco, he bought everything; the back catalogue, the brands, the equipment. We agreed not to go back into the business. Kara and I were happy with the price.

I wasn't so happy telling everyone, it was the hardest thing I'd ever done. A few were upset, some shrugged, thanked us and went off to find other things. Our buyer offered Andy, Becky, and Troy jobs, which they all took after some consideration, but the hardest part was losing Alice.

Our buyer wanted her and offered her a very tempting deal. I didn't try to stop her. We'd enjoyed two years together and she'd grown so much in that time. She loved what she was doing and wanted to continue.

"What are you going to do now?" Kara asked.
"I'm not sure," I replied. "There's no hurry."
I was having dinner with Kara and Gina a week or so after the sale had all gone through. We still hadn't taken it in, it had happened so fast.
"What about you?" I asked.
"Never have to work again," she said, grinning.
"No, but I want to do something. Something for me."
"Any ideas?"
"Yea, I have."
I was going to talk to someone who had become especially important to me.

"So, you're giving it all up?"
"Yes, pani Agata."
"Just like that?"

"Yes. It's all come rather suddenly."

Madame Górska and I had become friends. Was that the right word? No, probably not. She had welcomed me as she welcomed anyone who showed her a modicum of respect, and she didn't care who you were or what you did. Her shop was frequented by elderly ladies looking for old-fashioned foundation wear, all the way through to girls who worked in the sex industry and wanted more provocative items.

She wasn't cheap, and that limited the numbers coming through the doors. Even so, she worked hard and always seemed to be in her workroom. Since I met her, she'd made some beautiful things for me. Whenever I wore them, I felt special.

She'd seen my delight in her work, and she'd become something of a mother figure for me. The mother I wish I'd had. I called her pani Agata; a diminutive I was told she allowed few to use.

I was sitting on the edge of a counter, the only free space I could find. She was sitting at her worktop, hand-finishing an ordinary, everyday corset, but with the same attention to detail she gave everything she did. As we talked, she didn't look up, and occasionally she didn't reply because one stitch was giving her trouble. I knew now to wait; she'd reply when she was happy.

"What are you going to do now, Bella?"

"I want to do something different."

"No more naughty films?" She gave me a knowing grin.

"No."

"What would you like to do?"

"I'd like to do what you do."

"Make clothes?"

"No, make corsetry."

She gave me a hard look.

"Pah! Nobody wants it anymore, and nobody learns how to make it anymore."

"Teach me."

She sat motionless for a moment, then put her work down and wearily slid her glasses off her head. She put on the inevitable second pair so she could see me across the room and studied me for a while.

"Bella, I'm getting old. My eyes hurt every evening from this close work. It's time for me to retire. I learnt this from my aunt, but I've never trained anyone. I've made a decent living, but I couldn't afford to pay you. My clients are dying out."

"I'm not asking to be paid, I'm asking to learn. And you have plenty of clients."

"I don't have the time."

"If I helped out, we could make time."

We swapped objections and solutions a few more times, until we were both smiling; knowing it had become a game.

"Please think about it, pani Agata. I'm serious."

I became an apprentice corsetiere the following week. Madame Górska was dubious at first, but she was right about one thing. She was tired. Her movements had become painful and she was struggling with her eyesight. I soon found out why; she was resistant to change and didn't look after herself. It took me months to persuade her to let me help.

Eventually, I took her to the doctors. This led to a new hip which she did nothing but moan about for months. But after recovering, she was whizzing about the shop again. A visit to the opticians led to the first new glasses for what turned out to be years. A pair of bifocals produced more moans and groans, but sometimes I caught her looking across the room, moving from one lens to the other, and she smiled when she saw me watching her.

I fed her, too. Every day, I took something for us to eat at lunchtime. She turned her nose up at first but was soon asking what I'd brought today. I asked her to teach me some Polish dishes and we had fun cooking together, even though she always complained it was time we weren't working.

And all this time, I was learning. She only let me do the basic stuff to begin with, but I used the time to quietly tidy the shop, finding a home for everything. It was a treasure trove of material and accessories, much of it decades old.

She begrudgingly let me buy a good electric sewing machine and tutted over my shoulder as I tried to sew a seam straight enough to pass her inspection. One day when I returned to the shop after going out, I found her working on the electric machine. She looked up guiltily, and we soon had a second one, the old treadle machine being retired as a part of the window display.

The five years I spent working with pani Agata were the happiest of my life. I found I had a knack for needlework and sewing, but also design. My problem was my drawing; it was awful. I had all these ideas in my head but could never get them down on paper. I took a part-time course at a nearby design college, and although I never became as good as I wanted to be, I learnt how to show clients what I had in mind.

Those clients changed too. We still had Madame Górska's older customers; women she'd known for decades, and some of the working girls, particularly the dominatrices, many of whom I knew. But I also joined a BDSM group; the one Gina attended. Kara came along as well. We weren't professionals now and we wanted to enjoy our hobby, our lifestyle. Many of the people there became friends and customers.

I didn't find a soulmate in those years; I'm not even sure, looking back, I was seeking one. I did have some interesting relationships, all but one with me being firmly in charge. The one was a guy I met at a supplier; he was smart, funny, and not at all bothered about my past.

We were together for over a year and it could have got serious. But in the end, we knew my need for control wasn't going to work for him. He willingly tried everything, but it didn't do anything for him. We parted amicably and looking back, I'm not sure what I was doing. From the beginning, we knew he wasn't into my world. Perhaps I was having one final go at an ordinary adult relationship.

Change came suddenly, again. Pani Agata fell ill; she was diagnosed with cancer and faded quickly. Her passing was painful; far more than my own mother's had been. She had no family and near the end, I asked about her past.

"You don't want to hear my sad story," she said.

"I do, if you can tell me."

"My father was a diplomat before the war, in Paris. When it was clear war was coming, he knew it wasn't safe for us all to go back to Poland, being Jewish. When he was recalled, he left my mother in Paris and returned to Warsaw. They sent me to my aunt here in London. I was ten and I'd never met her.

"I never saw either of them again. My father was probably murdered early in the war, and my mother was rounded up in nineteen forty-two. She was both Polish and Jewish; she didn't stand a chance. She went home, but only to Treblinka to die."

There were tears as she told the story; tears from both of us. Hers for her parents, lost to hatred. Mine for a woman I'd come to love, and who was leaving me.

She had no family, but she wasn't friendless. Her funeral was a huge affair, and a joyous one after the solemn ceremony. I knew many of her friends and most of our clients attended as well. We did our best to honour her memory.

She told me shortly before her death she was leaving the house and business to me. I was astonished, but she brooked no argument. The day after the funeral, I sat in the shop and tears streamed down my face as I looked around the workroom. It held so many memories, the most stable memories of my life. I didn't know how I was going to carry on working there.

But I did, and I worked out a plan. I took on two apprentices myself. Amy and Tabby. They were both fresh out of college, and they knew all the basics. Training them was easy and they were willing learners. They were surprised by some of our customers but adapted quickly. Although we still served a dwindling number of older ladies, our younger clientele increased, and we catered to their needs.

My life had changed out of all recognition. I'd found my new niche and succeeded, but it was time to move on.

Epilogue

I've told you my story. I've left a few things out; you may not be interested in them, and I may not want to tell them. But there it is.

Kara and Gina remained my best friends and their relationship lasted. They had to move from the stable after Janos turned up on their doorstep, but Kara was able to buy a place and they found a beautiful warehouse conversion in Southwark. We're still close and meet often.

I decided to leave London. I was born and brought up there, but I wanted something quieter; somewhere to relax and ... what? Get away from the past? No, it's not as simple as that, I wasn't ashamed of anything I'd done. I'm not now. But I wanted to start again, somewhere I wasn't known and could live my life on my own terms.

I handed the business over to Amy and Tabby; they're still there. But all pani Agata's old customers are gone, and they cater to a high-end clientele wanting expensive underwear and something special. I visit when I'm in London and get real pleasure from their success.

I found peace here, in a house I could only have dreamt of when I was nineteen or twenty. I've spent time furnishing it and surrounding myself with things that make me happy. In pride of place is pani Agata's treadle sewing machine, in the window of my workroom. I see it every day, and it reminds me of the woman who I first saw hunched over it.

I live on my own terms now. I have used the name Helen since I moved here; it seemed a clean break from my past, at the time. Now, I'm not sure why I bothered, but it's too late to change it back. It would mean explaining too many things to too many people.

I still make corsetry, but only to a select group of friends and acquaintances who want the very best; indeed, want something many would consider way over the top. But I love putting my skills to the test.

After I moved, I found there was a gap in my life. I needed the world I'd come to love. It was hugely important to me and the lack of like-minded people left me feeling isolated. So, I was involved in setting up a fetish group. I've made many friends and although I'm not as involved as I was, the group seems to go from strength to strength.

I found a few interesting playmates, but none lasted. Then, four years ago, I met Penny. She had been in a relationship that ended, and a mutual friend thought we might be compatible. We spoke a couple of times and arranged to meet. Within a few minutes, we both knew we'd found something special.

And it is.

Very special.

Author's Note

I would like to thank all those involved in helping me bring this story to the page. You know who you are, and I will be eternally grateful.

If you've enjoyed this book, please think about leaving a review, either on the marketplace where you bought it or on one of the many book review sites, such as Goodreads. Reviews are helpful for both authors and other readers.

This novella is part of the Kinky Companions series. The first novel is Sally's Shadow, and if you haven't read it, why not try it? Helen features in the story from the second novel, New Temptations. I hope you'll join Sally, Marcus, and Lucy in their adventures.

To keep in touch with my writing, you can visit my website, or follow me on social media.

Website: www.alexmarkson.com
Twitter: @amarksonerotica
Facebook: @amarksonerotica
Goodreads: Alex Markson

Alex Markson
June 2020